Crime for Christmas

As Lesley Egan:

CRIME FOR CHRISTMAS
LITTLE BOY LOST
RANDOM DEATH
THE MISER
A CHOICE OF CRIMES
MOTIVE IN SHADOW
THE HUNTERS AND THE
  HUNTED
LOOK BACK ON DEATH
A DREAM APART
THE BLIND SEARCH
SCENES OF CRIME
PAPER CHASE
MALICIOUS MISCHIEF
IN THE DEATH OF A MAN
THE WINE OF VIOLENCE
A SERIOUS INVESTIGATION
THE NAMELESS ONES
SOME AVENGER, ARISE
DETECTIVE'S DUE
MY NAME IS DEATH
RUN TO EVIL
AGAINST THE EVIDENCE
THE BORROWED ALIBI
A CASE FOR APPEAL

As Elizabeth Linington:

SKELETONS IN THE CLOSET
CONSEQUENCE OF CRIME
NO VILLAIN NEED BE
PERCHANCE OF DEATH
CRIME BY CHANCE
PRACTISE TO DECEIVE
POLICEMAN'S LOT
SOMETHING WRONG
DATE WITH DEATH
NO EVIL ANGEL
GREENMASK!
THE PROUD MAN
THE LONG WATCH
MONSIEUR JANVIER

THE KINGBREAKER
ELIZABETH I (Ency. Brit.)

As Egan O'Neill:

THE ANGLOPHILE

As Dell Shannon:

CASE PENDING
THE ACE OF SPADES
EXTRA KILL
KNAVE OF HEARTS
DEATH OF A BUSYBODY
DOUBLE BLUFF
ROOT OF ALL EVIL
MARK OF MURDER
THE DEATH-BRINGERS
DEATH BY INCHES
COFFIN CORNER
WITH A VENGEANCE
CHANCE TO KILL
RAIN WITH VIOLENCE
KILL WITH KINDNESS
SCHOOLED TO KILL
CRIME ON THEIR HANDS
UNEXPECTED DEATH
WHIM TO KILL
THE RINGER
MURDER WITH LOVE
WITH INTENT TO KILL
NO HOLIDAY FOR CRIME
SPRING OF VIOLENCE
CRIME FILE
DEUCES WILD
STREETS OF DEATH
APPEARANCES OF DEATH
COLD TRAIL
FELONY AT RANDOM
FELONY FILE
MURDER MOST STRANGE
THE MOTIVE ON RECORD
EXPLOIT OF DEATH

Crime for Christmas

LESLEY EGAN

PUBLISHED FOR THE CRIME CLUB BY
DOUBLEDAY & COMPANY, INC.
GARDEN CITY, NEW YORK

All of the characters in this book
are fictitious, and any resemblance
to actual persons, living or dead,
is purely coincidental.

Library of Congress Cataloging in Publication Data
Egan, Lesley, 1921–
Crime for Christmas.
I. Title.
PS3562.I515C7   1983   813'.54
ISBN 0-385-19070-0

Library of Congress Catalog Card Number 83–11511
Copyright © 1983 by Doubleday & Company, Inc.
All Rights Reserved
Printed in the United States of America

This one again
is for
Doreen Tovey

Man is born unto trouble as the sparks fly upward.

Job 5:7

Crime for Christmas

CHAPTER 1

O'Connor marched into the detective office at Glendale head-quarters about the middle of the afternoon. Varallo was the sole occupant, reading a report. "Will you tell me, for God's sake," said O'Connor savagely, "why I ever thought police work would be interesting? My God, talk about monotony! I might as well be in an assembly plant screwing in bolt forty-six all day!" He perched a hip on the corner of Varallo's desk and lit a cigarette.

"For God's sake, don't complain of monotony," said Varallo. "You'll call down a spate of offbeat ones on us, Charles."

"I wouldn't much care," said O'Connor moodily. "At least it'd be a change. This new thing down—another damn fool punk kid, DOA on dope, and of course nowhere to go on it. Mother went out shopping this morning—he's twenty, out of work—came home and found he hadn't got up, looked at him and he's dead. There's a little stash of heroin left in a dresser drawer. She didn't have a clue that he was on dope, she says—no idea where he could have got it—my good God, anywhere on the street—or where he'd have got the money. He's got a little pedigree of possession. Nowhere to go."

"Write the report and file it," said Varallo.

"I get so damned tired of the stupid punks," said O'Connor. Absently he hitched up the .357 magnum in the shoulder holster. "Damn waste of time—go talk to his pals, probably users too, they don't know where he got it, oh, no, don't know nothin'. I get so damned tired."

"Just a thankless job," said Varallo wryly. "I've got some more of it. This pair of heisters, there's just nowhere to go. I've been downtown all morning with the latest victims, and they couldn't make any mug shots. They say Latin types, but they all look alike, and it was so fast, I just couldn't say."

"Those jewelry store heists. The way it goes," said O'Connor gloomily. "There was a time I thought of going in for law. I couldn't afford it." At this time of day his square bulldog face needed another shave, his chin was blue; as usual, his tie was crooked and his shirt rumpled. "Anything new gone down?" he added without much interest.

"I couldn't say, I just got back, but everybody else is out on something." And it was threatening to start raining again—gray and overcast. Last winter had brought them a spate of rain before Christmas, and then nothing the rest of the wet season in southern California; this winter had started out bringing early heavy rains again. This first week of December had seen a torrential three-day downpour and then a couple of gray, dry days; now the forecast was for more rain.

Sergeant Joe Katz and Detective John Poor came in, shed their coats at the door, and sat down at their respective desks. "And I'll tell you something," said Katz bitterly to Varallo. "Sooner or later these jokers are going to end up with a homicide charge, and it'll be your baby. And good luck to you on it. There's no making head or tail of the damn thing—just no goddamned handle at all—my good God, this makes fifteen of them—fifteen in just under a month and no goddamned leads at all. And sooner or later—" He slumped back in his desk chair and shut his eyes.

Poor said, "All elderly people. Scared and upset. And the same pair—we keep hearing the same story—but damn all on any leads." They were both looking discouraged and tired.

There was silence for a few minutes in the big square room; O'Connor smoked and brooded; Varallo finished reading the report; Katz and Poor sat and stared into space. The tall windows began to stream with gray rain. Varallo sat back in his desk chair, lit a cigarette, and emitted a long column of smoke. "The thankless job," he said. "We go through the motions, Charles." And then his gaze went past O'Connor, and he added roughly, "What the hell are you doing here?"

Their female detective, Delia Riordan, was just coming into the big communal office. She took off her trench coat and draped it across the back of her desk chair; she gave them a faint smile. "What's the point of just going home, Vic? I'm all right. I

wanted to finish typing that report—tomorrow's my day off."
She sat down at her desk and took the cover off her typewriter.

They all watched her a little uneasily, not knowing what to
say. There had been a time when O'Connor had bitterly resented being banded with a female detective, even one with
the valuable experience on the LAPD; but she was a good girl,
Delia, a good police officer. In the four years and more she'd
been with them, they'd come to appreciate her. These last few
years she hadn't been as reluctant to show her femininity: her
dark brown hair was longer and waved loosely, she wore a little
more makeup and neat tailored dresses instead of pantsuits. She
was really a very good-looking girl, Delia, not looking her age—
which they happened to know was thirty-two—with a slim, neat
figure; if she wasn't pretty in the ordinary sense, she had good
regular features, a smooth, milky skin, good blue eyes. She was
one of them; they all liked her.

"You should have gone home," said Varallo.

"Why? No point, Vic. I'm OK." Delia bent over the typewriter and began to transcribe her notes.

"It's supposed to go on raining tomorrow," said O'Connor.

"And the traffic is something else," said Katz. "All the Christmas shoppers. It took me half an hour to get back from Kenneth
Road."

Delia heard the desultory exchange of talk vaguely. She
hunched over the typewriter, deciphering the notes she'd
taken yesterday, aware that the men were watching her co-
vertly, aware of their silent sympathy—but of course, she
thought, it wasn't necessary, not at all.

There were stopping places in life, she thought, where you
came to the end of one thing and started on another phase, as it
were. You could say that the place she'd got to today marked the
end of her whole life up to now. All those long years of proving
herself as an LAPD policewoman, the long hours of study ac-
quiring all the useful skills to make her more efficient, the fluent
Spanish, the courses in police science—most of the time working the swing shift, so unavoidably she had lost contact with
friends—you couldn't say it had all been for nothing, but of
course it had all been for Alex. It had had to be the thankless,

sordid job, for Alex. Alex Riordan, losing his first wife after twenty years of childless marriage, marrying a girl half his age only to lose her in childbirth a year later. Delia didn't know much about her mother. They had managed somehow, she and Alex, with a succession of housekeepers, until the year he was sixty-five and Delia was thirteen. He'd been full of plans for her first time of entering the junior target pistol competition—he'd started her with a gun on her seventh birthday. Then, just two days before his official retirement, he'd gone out on his last call—Captain Alex Riordan, Robbery-Homicide, LAPD—and taken the bank robber's bullet in the spine. That had been a bad time for a while, and then they'd found Steve—ex-Sergeant Steve McAllister, LAPD, just short of twenty-five years' service when he lost a leg in an accident: a widower with a married daughter. The three of them had been together for fourteen and a half years—the new leg hadn't hampered Steve from manipulating Alex's wheelchair, and Alex had always liked to cook. Of course, of course, it had had to be this job for Alex—she was all he'd ever had. This job—pretending to be the son Alex had never had.

Neil had seen that from the first, and hadn't he tried to make her see it—stubborn, blind, foolish Delia resisting him all the way. She and Isabel Fordyce had been best friends all through school, and Neil not really the superior elder brother—a friend, until he was something else. How desperately she had held out against him, blindly committed to the all-important job for Alex —and how they had hated each other, of course—the two strong characters.

And it hadn't been until three and a half years ago that she had, in one devastating moment, realized the truth: that the little victory she had won was less than meaningless. Neil coming to say good-bye and good luck—and she had known, starkly, that she had nothing at all in return for the sacrifice of resisting him. In the years of hard work on the job, all her friends had drifted away. She hadn't even talked on the phone with Isabel for a year before that last time of seeing Neil; and a month after that she'd had the last letter from Isabel—Isabel so happily married, with three children now: the note telling her noncommittally that Neil had married a Spanish girl he'd met in Ecuador. He'd been directing an archaeological dig there for the University of Arizona.

So it had come to her that it had all been for nothing. The promise of a meaningful life, a woman's life, exchanged for a mess of pottage. And most frighteningly, she had suddenly seen her two idols, Alex and Steve, as two rather commonplace men of narrow interests and little knowledge outside their dreary job.

So all that was left to her was that job. It was nothing of any importance to her as a woman; but if all that was left to her was the sterile job, it was something, a job she could do well. And Alex was proud of her; Alex and Steve loved her.

And then that had changed, all in a moment, like the patterns changing in a kaleidoscope. It was two and a half years ago that Alex had had the crippling stroke, and he had been in the convalescent home ever since, helpless and paralyzed. There had been good days and bad days: sometimes he knew her; increasingly of late, he hadn't. When it had become evident that he was never coming home again, Steve had gone back to Denver to live with his daughter; he wasn't much of a letter writer, and Delia seldom heard from him.

And then, after the long, heartbreaking time, last Friday Alex had slipped away to some other place. One thing this long time of living alone had given Delia was time for reading for pleasure, and in these last years she had read voraciously; and she no longer believed that Alex had been dissolved into nothing: there was too much evidence on that, which had nothing to do with orthodox churches. He had gone somewhere else, the Alex she had known in his prime—irascible, stubborn, opinionated, and tough—and he was all right. Somewhere. But he had been violently antireligious, and she couldn't have inflicted on him any kind of orthodox service.

He had been cremated this morning, and she had accompanied the urn with the ashes up to the mausoleum at Rose Hills cemetery this afternoon. The Varallos and O'Connor had offered to go with her, and she had said to them, what was the point? It wouldn't make any difference to Alex. It was all over, and the entire thirty-two years with Alex had decided the whole course of her life. She couldn't mourn for him; she could only be thankful he was released from the frustration and misery; and she couldn't mourn for herself, for it had been her own stubbornness that had kept her on the course which had left her with only the sterile job for the rest of her life.

She smoked too many cigarettes, laboring over the typed report: the report on the heist that had gone down Saturday night, the latest in a series probably pulled by the same pair. There wasn't much meat in it. Varallo had taken the victims downtown yesterday to look at mug shots, and they hadn't made any. This report would get filed away with the other reports of similar heists, and it was unlikely that any charges would ever be brought; but the paperwork went on forever, and it was something to occupy her mind. Alex, she thought wryly, would thoroughly approve of her going back to the office right away.

She finished the report at five-thirty, separated the triplicate forms, filed one to be sent to the captain's office, filed the other two, and decided to go home early. O'Connor had gone back to his cubbyhole of an office; Katz and Poor were studying reports; Varallo was on the phone; and nobody else had come back.

It had started raining in earnest, a workmanlike steady drizzle. Delia found a plastic rain hood in her bag, went out the back door of the station to the parking lot, and ducked into the car in a hurry. It was slow driving in the dark down to Brand Boulevard, across town through Atwater into Hollywood. The traffic was thick, and she was held up through two changes of traffic lights at Riverside Drive, but eventually got past the intersection and turned off Los Feliz down to Waverly Place.

As she slid the Ford into the garage, she thought vaguely that she had better put the house up for sale. Ridiculous to go on living in the huge, two-story old Spanish house with its four bedrooms, and it had long been clear of any mortgage. It was in a good residential area and with prices inflated would sell for a good deal more than Alex had paid for it. She thought, a nice little apartment somewhere closer to work, not so much housework, more cheerful. There hadn't been anybody to welcome her home for a long time, but the old house seemed somehow more dank and dark and empty today. She went around quickly turning on lights; she looked into the freezer and selected a TV dinner at random. Tomorrow was her day off, and she would do all the usual things: have her hair washed and set, do a laundry, change the bed. Sometimes she and Laura Varallo met for lunch, but the forecast said more rain and it would be a nuisance for Laura.

She picked out one of her library books at random to read over dinner.

Varallo came home to the house on Hillcroft Road at six-thirty. A high wind had got up, and the old trees lining the street were bending and tossing; it had turned cold. When he came in the back door, the kitchen was invitingly warm and Laura was setting the table in the dining room. "You're late—I'll bet the traffic was murder."

"Christmas shoppers," said Varallo, kissing her. "Delia came back to the office. I wish she hadn't. It seems—"

"Why?" asked Laura. She surveyed him calmly, his lovely brown-haired Laura, looking serene. "Let her handle it her own way, Vic. She's been alone, to all intents and purposes, for quite a while. She'll be all right."

"Yes, I suppose so," he said doubtfully.

"Don't fuss her. Delia's all right," said Laura. "Do you want a drink before dinner?"

"Maybe I deserve one. We're never going to get anywhere on those damned heists, and there's another homicide, not that it's anything to work, just another idiotic kid overdosed on dope. The autopsy will say what, and there won't be a hope of finding out where he got it."

"Go and sit down and relax. I built a fire. I'll bring you a drink."

Varallo went into the living room to be pounced on by the children. A year ago Ginevra had demanded to be read to; these days, in first grade, she wanted to read to him and was gratifyingly proficient at it. Johnny, at four, was glib on the alphabet but still wanted the bedtime stories. There was a crackling fire on the hearth, and the majestic gray tabby Gideon Algernon Cadwallader was basking somnolently on the hearth rug. Varallo sat down in his big armchair, accepted the brandy and soda gratefully, and looked at Laura over Ginevra's blond head where she snuggled in his lap.

"I just wish she hadn't come in. I suppose it's silly."

"Yes," said Laura calmly. "From all we know, he was very much the career cop, Vic. He'd have wanted her to. She hadn't anywhere else to go, after all."

"I suppose not."

O'Connor hunched his shoulders against the rain, getting out to open the driveway gates, ran the Ford into the garage, latched the gates, and dived for the back door. It was raining steadily. In the service porch he was greeted exuberantly by the outsize blue Afghan, Maisie, and said, "Down, damn it." He shed his raincoat and hat. "I'm damn sick of this weather."

"We're spoiled," said Katharine. "Think of what the rest of the country's getting—snow and ice. I won't ask if you had a good day."

O'Connor kissed her and said, "Don't. Delia came back to the office."

"And why not?" asked Katharine reasonably. "Nobody at home for her."

"Well, no," said O'Connor. "It just seemed—queer."

"You leave Delia alone," said Katharine. "Do you want a drink before dinner?"

O'Connor sneezed and said thickly, "Yes."

"You aren't coming down with a cold?"

"No, no, I'm all right."

"Well, you'd better not, or Vince'll get it."

"Such a very sympathetic wife. I just sometimes feel," said O'Connor, "that I'd have done better to try to get through that law course. This goddamned job—day in, day out, the same goddamn stupid things going on, the mindless punks and the thugs doing what comes naturally—I swear to God, Katy, I get so damn tired of the whole goddamned mess—"

Katharine surveyed him amusedly. "You'd be bored stiff in any other job. Relax and forget it. Dinner in half an hour."

Grumbling, O'Connor built himself a drink, ripped his tie loose, and went into the living room, where four-year-old Vincent Charles was crawling over the carpet making realistic engine noises for a toy fire truck. He erupted at O'Connor joyously.

"Daddy—tell the story about Santa Claus again! Mama says we going to have a big Christmas tree—bigger than last Christmas but I don't bemember last Christmas—"

O'Connor collapsed into his armchair, and Maisie tried to climb into his lap. Vince shoved her away and got there first. "Tell again about Santa Claus, Daddy!"

O'Connor sipped his drink, sneezed, and hoped uneasily that he wasn't coming down with a cold. "Well, he's a very good, kind saint, and he loves all little children—"

"We seed him at the store downtown—Mama and me—and I don't think he loves everybody," said Vince. "He was comin' out of the door into the store and he was talkin' to a man and he said, 'Damn these kids.' Why do you think he loves everybody, Daddy?"

"Well," said O'Connor. "Well, he was just dressed up like Santa Claus, Vince. The real Santa Claus really does love everybody and all little children."

"How do you know?" asked Vince reasonably.

The night watch came on—Bob Rhys and Jim Harvey; it was Dick Hunter's night off. They got their first call, to a heist, at a quarter past nine, and both went out on it. As they came out the back door of the station, the wind was blowing a gale, and it had turned colder.

"Supposed to rain again tomorrow," said Rhys, sliding the key into the ignition. "If you ask me, it's too cold." In southern California it was seldom very cold when it was raining, but the last few years had brought some unprecedented weather patterns.

The address the squad had called in was on North Central. It was a little jewelry store sandwiched between a dress shop and a dry cleaner's in a half block of small stores. Rhys looked at it, getting out of the car, and said, "Oh-oh. You want to bet?"

"No bets," said Harvey dispiritedly. They went in. The squad-car man was listening to a little fat man who was talking excitedly, waving his arms.

"These are the detectives, Mr. Polanski. You just tell them all about it."

"Sure, sure. These two guys came in, and it's just before closing, see, I don't keep open past six usually, I'm open to nine Fridays is all, but it's Christmas season, people shopping out all hours, you never know when you make a sale, I stay open to nine up to Christmas, see? It was slow, I only had a couple of customers in and no big sale, just a cheap wristwatch and a Hoover High class ring—it's maybe a quarter of nine, I'm about to call it a night and go home—these two guys come in and put a gun on me, they clean out two cases of stuff, make me unlock the doors, and by damn, it's a hell of a big gun, I'm not about to put up a fight, I got a family to think about—"

"Yes, sir," said Rhys. "Can you describe the men, Mr. Polanski?"

"Sure, sure I can—they were both Mexes, Latin types, you know? Pretty young, maybe twenty-five, one of 'em had a little mustache—they didn't talk English so good, had accents, you know? I'd have to look at the books, see what they got away with —some diamond rings, earrings, gold bracelets, God knows— two cases full, those two cases right there—"

"Do you think you could recognize either of them?"

Polanski gave a massive shrug. "You want me to go look at your mug shots? I don't know. A lot of those types, they look alike. They were only in here three, four minutes. I don't know as I could pick either of them."

"Did you see a car?"

"Naw—they're in and out. If they had a car, it wasn't right outside, and I wasn't about to follow them outside—they came and went, and I locked the door and called for cops—sure, sure, I can tell you what they got away with after I look over the books—"

They spent another half hour talking to him, but that was all that emerged. It was about all that had so far emerged on this pair of heisters in the last three weeks. They had hit seven jewelry shops more or less in the central area of Glendale; on each job they had hit just before closing time, when there were no customers in. A couple of the shops had been fairly high-class places with quality merchandise, and they had got away with quite a respectable haul so far. None of it had turned up at any pawnshops, which probably said that the heisters were pros who knew a tame fence. A couple of the victims had pored over the books of mug shots but hadn't picked out any except tentatively, and two of those they'd picked, chased down by the day watch, had proved to have alibis, and a third was doing time in Susanville. This looked like another dead end.

They asked Polanski to come into the station tomorrow to sign a statement and to make up a list of what the heisters had got away with. There wasn't much for them to do on it but type a report. They got back to the station at a little after ten o'clock; it wasn't raining now, but the wind was still high and the air was chill and damp.

As they came in the back door of the station, the fluorescent lights flickered once and from outside came the sudden, steady, loud rumble of an engine. "I'll be damned," said Harvey. "The power's gone." That was something that didn't happen often in the city, a blackout of power; but it did happen occasionally, and of all places in the city, a police station had to have electric power to operate. Out there at the rear of the station, the big generator had rumbled into life automatically as the power failed; running on diesel fuel, it would provide power for the station as long as the blackout lasted.

"This wind," said Rhys. "I'll bet there's a line down somewhere around."

Upstairs, he started to type the report; there wasn't much in it. And if there was a line down, the power company got a crew on it without delay; half an hour later the generator gave a last thud and subsided into silence, and the lights didn't even flicker.

At midnight they were sitting talking desultorily, bored as the night dragged by. Traffic might be busy out on the streets; in the first week of December people were already out partying and visiting, and at least up to midnight traffic was heavier than usual.

"This job can be a drag," said Harvey through a yawn. "The rest of the family's going up to my sister's in Fresno for Christmas—I'll be alone. I guess about the only celebration I'll have is going to church on Christmas Eve."

"We don't usually do much anyway," said Rhys. "Just the two of us." He was a bachelor and lived with his mother, who wished he'd get married and start a family. "Yeah, we cuss about night watch, but it can be a lot more peaceful than the legwork the day boys come in for. Mother usually has a couple of the neighbors in for drinks and snacks, that's about all."

"I might put in for a couple of days out of my sick leave."

At ten past twelve Communications relayed a call, an address on Sonora Avenue, a 459. This time they took Harvey's car.

It was, as expectable in that area, a modest old single house, stucco with a red tile roof. The porch light was on, the squad parked in front. Rhys pushed the bell and the uniformed man, Steiner, let them in. "It's another of these funny ones," he said. "I covered a couple of them—doesn't seem to be any handle to it, from what I hear. This is Mrs. Minturn— These are the detectives, ma'am. You tell them just what you've been telling me."

"Yes, oh yes, of course—it was just terrible—I was so frightened—they didn't hurt me or anything, but I was never so frightened in my life—" She was a thin little old lady with gray hair wildly disheveled; she clutched an old blue chenille bathrobe around her, and her blue-veined old hands were trembling. "I'd gone to bed—I usually go to bed after I've heard the eleven o'clock news—I don't know what time it was, but I wasn't asleep yet, when the doorbell rang—I was sort of flustered, you know, that late at night, but I got up—well, if I'd stopped to think, I'd have realized that if anything was wrong with the family someone would have phoned—my son or daughter—but I went and switched on the porch light, and of course I'm always careful, there's a chain on the door, I just opened it a crack and said, 'Who is it?'—and the man said it was police—he said my name, he said, 'Mrs. Minturn?'—and I said yes, and he said it was police, and there was a prowler in my backyard and they wanted to come in to use my phone—"

Which was just what Rhys and Harvey had expected to hear. "And so naturally I opened the door and unhooked the chain— you have to help the police—and I just had time to see there were two of them, and one of them had a uniform on—when they pushed right in, and they had these awful masks on, stretched tight over their faces, and one of them said they wouldn't hurt me, I was just to be quiet—and he showed me a horrible big knife, and made me sit on the sofa—and the other one started going all through the house, he brought things and put them by the front door, my new toaster oven and the portable radio and the TV from the bedroom—and he took all the money out of my handbag—I'd just cashed my Social Security check—" Suddenly she began to cry gently. "That was bad enough, but they found the wristwatch I'd got for Ardeth—my granddaughter, she's ten, I got it for her for Christmas, it was the first Christmas present I'd bought, I'd saved up for it, it's a nice one, a Bulova—and they took that too—and now I won't be able to get any presents for the family—"

Rhys gave her a little time and asked, "Could you make any guess about their ages—their size?"

"Oh, they were young—and they were both big—bigger than you." She eyed Rhys, thin and middle-sized, a little doubtfully. "Their voices sounded young."

"Did they call each other by any names?"

"N-no, I don't think so. They didn't talk much. The one just stayed by me all the while, with that awful knife, and the other one put all my things by the front door and then he carried it all out—I suppose—and put it in a car, and then the one with the knife said I'd been nice and quiet so everything was fine—and he went out too—and oh, oh, if they just hadn't taken Ardeth's watch! The rest was bad enough—all my money for the month, and all the rest—but it was the only Christmas present I'd got yet, and I still had to get presents for Jean and Bill and Roy and Linda and the other children—and now I can't, with no money—"

Rhys and Harvey looked at each other. "The uniform, Mrs. Minturn," said Harvey. "Did it look like a police uniform?"

"I don't know," she said with a little sob. "It was just a uniform. Like a soldier's, you know. And he had on a cap—like a soldier's cap, with a sort of stiff front."

"Like a bill? Like an officer's cap?"

"Yes, like that. But I couldn't see their faces—they had these awful masks on—oh, if they just hadn't taken Ardeth's watch!"

"How much money did they get, could you tell us?"

"It was about five hundred dollars—I had a little left from last month—"

"Did they take any jewelry, anything else?"

She shook her head. "When they went—I couldn't do anything for a little while—I'd been so frightened—but I knew I had to call the police—and then I looked to see if they'd stolen my engagement ring—I don't wear it much anymore, but I know it's a good diamond, Harry paid a lot for it back then, what seemed a lot—prices now—but they hadn't taken any of the jewelry, not that I've got a lot, but there's my engagement ring and two other diamond rings that belonged to my mother, and a gold bracelet set with garnets, and an opal ring that was Aunt Louise's—they didn't take any of it."

"You live here alone, Mrs. Minturn? Do you have relatives in town?"

"Oh yes," she said. She was trying gallantly to get hold of herself, to stop crying. "Yes. Harry—my husband—died five years ago. Of course, it's been a little hard—I don't drive, I sold the car—but the bus is pretty close, and my daughter Jean takes me shopping once a week, on Saturdays when she's not working, she works at a beauty shop—yes, she and Bill live in Burbank, and my son Roy lives in Eagle Rock—"

"You'd better let us call them, Mrs. Minturn. They'll be concerned about what's happened. Are you feeling all right?— Like us to call a doctor?"

"No, I'm all right," she said. "My heart's as sound as can be—I take pills for high blood pressure, but there's nothing else wrong with me. I expect I'd better call Roy—he'll have a fit— but nobody could say I'm careless, they all know I'm perfectly capable of living alone and managing—only for goodness' sake, when they said police, well, naturally you trust the police—"

"How many does that make?" asked Rhys in the car.

"I haven't counted. The day boys have been doing the spadework. Too many."

"The same damn MO. They know the names—say police, or fire—houses, apartments—two of them, and the uniform—how the hell do they know the names?" said Rhys savagely.

"It's a bastard," said Harvey. "It'll be driving the day boys

nuts. And the anonymous loot—the cash, the small appliances—
I think this is the fourteenth or fifteenth."

It was another report to write, and they didn't get another
call to the end of the shift.

"Talk about a bastard to work!" said Sergeant Joe Katz passionately on Tuesday morning. "And I swear to God, Varallo,
sooner or later one of the poor old victims is going to drop dead
of a stroke or a heart attack and it'll turn into a case for you."
Nominally speaking, the detectives were assigned to categories
—Varallo, Delia, Jeff Forbes, and Gil Gonzales to Robbery-
Homicide; O'Connor, Lew Wallace, and Leo Boswell to Narco;
Katz and Poor to Burglary. In practice, being shorthanded, they
all handled whatever came along.

"How in hell do these jokers know the names?" said Poor.
"Fifteen times they've pulled the same job—the elderly people
living alone—apartments and houses—in a couple of the apartments there's been a name on the mailbox, but no Mr., Mrs., or
Miss—on the houses nothing. In every case these jokers have
used a name—all the likelier the people will open doors to
them, naturally—Mr. Smith, this is the police—"

"Fifteen times!" said Katz. "Fifteen times in a month! The
same damn MO—the name, police, the masks, and they take
cash, small appliances, but no jewelry—the uniform—no car
spotted, of course—but what the hell is the common denominator? How the hell are these people connected?—there's got to
be some connection when the burglars know them by name! So
far there's just nothing—we started to look when number nine
showed up—club affiliations, churches, name it, there's nothing
in common—and it's all over the city, different addresses in all
sorts of neighborhoods—it's crazy. There's just no sense to it at
all, and no leads."

"A bastard to work," said Poor. And then he looked past Katz
and added, "Well, where did that come from?"

Varallo looked up. In the doorway of the communal detective
office there was a dog.

CHAPTER 2

It was a small black, woolly dog with a round head and a stub of a tail. It advanced into the big office confidently and came up to O'Connor, wagging its tail. "Well, where the hell did you come from?" said O'Connor, bending to pat the woolly head. "You're a funny-looking little mutt." The dog went on to Forbes, sniffing interestedly at his trousers, and then to Katz, and then Varallo. It seemed pleased to make new friends; the stub tail wagged and wagged.

Varallo got on the phone to the desk. "Listen, how'd this dog get in?"

"What dog?" asked Sergeant Bill Dick. "I haven't seen any dog."

"Well, there's one up here."

"Oh hell," said Dick, "that's funny, but I suppose it could have got in when the citizen came in, I wouldn't notice. I've been talking to this guy for the last fifteen minutes, he came in to complain about his trash-collection bill, and it took me a while to convince him it's nothing to do with us, he'll have to see the Department of Water and Power. I didn't see any dog, for God's sake."

"Well, just a second," said Varallo. "Come here, pooch." The dog came over, wagging its tail and grinning, and he investigated. There was a collar and a tag. "There's a name on the tag, Beal, and a phone number. You'd better call and tell them the dog's here. No point in calling the pound."

"OK, will do," said Dick amiably. The little dog was making the rounds of all the men in the office, friendly and happy.

"Kind of a cute little thing," said Katz. He took up Rhys's typed report again. "These damned burglaries—just nowhere to go."

"And another heist in that series," said Gil Gonzales, "no damn leads. This Polanski is supposed to come in and make a statement, but there won't be a damned thing in it by the night report, just more of what we've heard before. Damn all." He stroked his neat little mustache absently. All too many of the heists got filed away in Pending.

The dog had settled down contentedly under Katz's desk and was scratching vigorously behind one ear. The phone rang on Poor's desk and he picked it up. "Poor. OK, we're on it." He looked over at Katz. "New one down, lady just came home and found she's had a burglar."

"Hell," said Katz resignedly. "I suppose we'd better go and look at it." They went out together, collecting their coats from the rack inside the door. A couple of minutes later Dick called Varallo back.

"I got hold of this Mrs. Beal, it's her dog, she'll be right over to pick it up, she just lives a couple of blocks up on Isabel, she didn't know the dog had got out of the yard."

"Fine," said Varallo. "It's a cute little dog." He'd just put the phone down when it shrilled at him and he picked it up again. "Sergeant Varallo."

"You've got a homicide call," said the voice from Communications downstairs, and added the address, Everett Street.

"OK," said Varallo, and crooked a finger at Gonzales. "Here we go again. Another body to look at." They collected their coats from the rack and started downstairs. It was another gray day, drizzling very slightly.

As they left the office, the phone was ringing in O'Connor's cubbyhole; gregarious soul that he was, O'Connor rather resented that private office and was oftener to be found preempting somebody's desk in the big detective office. He went down to answer it, and Dick said, "I just had a call from an LAPD lieutenant, he wants to talk to somebody on Narco business, said he'd be here in half an hour."

"All right, all right, shoot him up when he gets here."

Ten minutes later a woman came into the detective office and said, "The man downstairs said she was up here—Rosie, oh, there she is—I'm so terribly sorry she bothered you—" She was a middle-aged woman, thin and nondescript, with graying brown hair; she was bundled up in a fake fur coat. "Rosie, naughty girl, come here!" The little dog trotted over to her and she scooped her up in her arms. "I'm so sorry—but of all the funny things, her coming to the police station! I take her on walks sometimes and we've been past here. The landlord said I could keep her because she's so little, and the side yard's fenced, but the other tenants are so careless about the gate—"

Jeff Forbes had stood up politely. "It's all right, ma'am, it's just lucky she wasn't run over or picked up by the pound."

"Oh *yes*, and I do apologize. So funny, her coming here—" She brought out a leash, snapped it onto the dog's collar. "Come on, Rosie, we're going home." She led the dog out. In the doorway she nearly collided with a man just coming in, a short, fat man who looked around and asked, "Is this where I'm supposed to come? My name's Polanski, I got held up last night, and the cop said to come in here and sign a statement—"

"Yes, sir," said Forbes. "That's right. Come in and sit down."

The address on Everett was an old four-family apartment house. The squad car was parked outside, and the uniformed man Steiner was waiting for the detectives. He said to Varallo and Gonzales, "It's a goddamned mess." There was a woman sitting in the backseat of the squad. "This is Mrs. Farley, she found them, it's her brother." From the glimpse they had, the woman was young and blond. She looked up at them past the open door of the squad and said, "Could you call my husband?— Bill Farley, he works at Webster's Men's Store in the Galleria— could you call him for me, please?"

"Surely, ma'am," said Steiner. "We'll be glad to."

"Oh, my God, if he'd only waited, if he'd only hung on—Bill was pretty sure he could get him that job at the furniture store —we'd been helping out as much as we could—"

"It's upstairs, the left rear," said Steiner. "There doesn't seem to be anybody else home in the place, and she says there's no manager on the premises."

Varallo and Gonzales climbed uncarpeted stairs and found the door to the left rear apartment open. In a small, shabbily furnished living room, there was a body on the couch: the body of a thin, dark young man in pajamas and bathrobe. His throat had been cut, and there was a lot of blood all over his upper body and on the couch and floor. A narrow-bladed kitchen knife lay under his right hand where his arm had slid down to trail on the floor. The blood was dry, and he'd been dead for a while, at least since last night.

Gonzales said, "There's a note on the desk."

"They usually leave one." The note was centered on a gimcrack little desk under the front window; they bent to read it without touching it. It was a penciled scrawl on a sheet torn from a cheap tablet.

Dear Jenny and Bill, I'm sorry to make you this trouble but I figure it's the only thing to do, don't seem either of us ever get jobs again, nothing for Ruth and the kid for Christmas, I don't see any way but this and we wouldn't take charity even if we starved, I guess it's best to take Ruth and the boy too, to save any more misery, so good-bye.

In silence Varallo straightened up and looked at the open door on the other side of the room. It led to a small, square bedroom, and the other two were in there; a young dark-haired woman on the bed, and a little boy about two years old in a crib. Both were wearing nightclothes; both had their throats cut, and the room was a shambles of dried blood.

"Sometime last night," said Varallo.

"The hell of a thing," said Gonzales.

But it was a straightforward thing; they wouldn't be calling out the lab on this one. File the report, and there'd be autopsies and a quick inquest. They went downstairs again. Steiner said, "I called in and asked the desk to notify the husband. What a hell of a mess."

Varallo bent to the squad. "Mrs. Farley? If you feel up to it, we'd like to ask you a couple of questions."

She was sitting up now, clutching a wadded handkerchief. She said thickly, "Yes, all right."

"That's your brother? What's his name?"

"Burt—Burt Fuller. And Ruth and Donnie. Oh God, he didn't need to—do that—oh God, if he'd just held on—Bill was sure he could get him that job if he'd just waited—but it was on account of Christmas, he'd been saying over and over, nothing for Christmas for Ruth and Donnie—he'd been out of work for months, and the unemployment insurance ran out—we couldn't help much—they'd both been trying and trying to get jobs—if he'd just hung on a while longer—oh God."

The husband arrived presently, a good-looking young fellow driving up in an old Chevy, and they let him take her home, and waited for the morgue wagon. Steiner said, "I suppose you'll have to find out who the landlord is and break the news. Hell of a mess to clean up." He went back on tour, and when the bodies had been carted off, Varallo and Gonzales went back to the station to write the report.

"Well, I wasn't home," said Mrs. Marjorie Kohler. She was a big, rawboned woman with prominent china blue eyes and an aggressive jaw. She looked at thin, dark Katz and sandy, nondescript Poor as if they were responsible for the whole thing. "I spent the night at my daughter's, I'd been there for dinner, and when it started to rain pretty bad they said I'd better stay over, it wasn't as if I had to get to work early, I'm on a split shift, don't have to go in till one. And I came home an hour ago to find all this mess—my God, what a mess—and he said—" She looked at the uniformed man—"not to touch anything—but what I can see, the toaster oven's gone, and the transistor radio, and all my good jewelry—and I've got good dead-bolt locks on both doors, but—"

"Other ways to get in, Mrs. Kohler," said Katz. In fact, he and Poor hadn't had to look twice to spot how the burglar had got in; there was a screen pried out of the rear window in the back bedroom, and the window smashed. The house was an old frame bungalow on a block of similar places; with all the noise the wind had been making last night, the neighbors wouldn't have heard anything.

"See if the lab can turn up anything," said Poor. Katz agreed and went out to the squad to call up somebody from the lab. The mobile van arrived fifteen minutes later with Rex Burt and Gene Thomsen; they started to dust surfaces.

Katz and Poor had shepherded Mrs. Kohler into the living room. "We'd like a description of what's missing," said Katz.

She obliged them readily. A brand new toaster oven, a GE portable transistor radio, a twelve-inch TV, the jewelry a little miscellany—a diamond ring, gold earrings, garnet ring, antique gold bracelet—a modest little haul as burglaries went. Katz and Poor had looked at a lot of burglaries; the rate was sky high and climbing the last couple of years; and a glance at this one had told them this and that right away. It had been somebody working alone, and they could guess why he had picked this place to break in. The single garage had been empty, no car parked in the drive, the garage door open: no outside lights on, he could guess there was nobody home. It was just the run-of-the-mill burglary; in the usual hurry he had dumped out drawers and left the expectable mess.

"I don't suppose there's any chance I'll get anything back even if you catch him," said Mrs. Kohler resentfully.

"Well, you never know," said Poor. The jewelry might show up at a pawnshop. This probably hadn't been a big-time operator who'd know a tame fence, and it wasn't very valuable jewelry. They'd add the description to the hot list sent to all pawnbrokers.

They left the lab men still poking around and went back to the station. They were less concerned about this, just another spur-of-the-minute burglary, than the mystery of the series of burglaries in the same pattern. While Poor typed the report, Katz went back over all those reports and came up empty again. Fifteen of them, damn it, he thought—counting Mrs. Minturn last night—since the second week of November. And while they followed a set pattern, the same MO with a couple of variations, there wasn't any common denominator. The same two men, by all the descriptions, and all the victims had been elderly; but the addresses were all over the city, widespread. In every case they'd known the victims' names, used the same pretext to get them to open the door. Even that had been the precise MO— where the victims lived in a single house, they'd announced themselves as police, the prowler in the backyard, let us in to use your phone. Where it was an apartment, they'd been firemen evacuating the building. The respectable elderly people had willingly opened the doors, been faced with the stocking masks, the knife, the promise not to harm. In every case but one, the victim had lived alone; the exception was an ancient couple in an old house on the outskirts of the city, both semi-invalids and, like the others, easily intimidated. The rest of the pattern—the burglars had gone first for any cash in the place, and in every case they had passed up any jewelry, taking only the small appliances, cameras. Last night had been the sole break in that pattern, when they'd taken the new wristwatch— and it wouldn't be identifiable, an anonymous Bulova.

The biggest mystery, of course, was how they knew the names. Only five of the victims had lived in apartments, and while the mailboxes in the lobby had been labeled with names, they hadn't identified the names as Mr., Mrs., or Miss; but the burglars had confidently sung out the labels. Mrs. Abrams, Miss Jacoby, Mr. Gaddis—and at the houses, there'd been no names displayed. And none of those people had anything in common at all; they lived in widely different areas of the city, they didn't know each other, didn't attend the same church or belong to the same social groups of any kind. There wasn't any link at all. How the hell had the burglars known the names?—to pick out the elderly, solitary victims, such easy prey? That was about all they did have in common; they had all been elderly, mostly living alone. Some of them had relatives around about, some had none. All of them had been drawing Social Security: a few had other pensions; one had been a retired army officer.

There were just no leads at all. Katz shuffled reports, rereading them for the dozenth time. According to three of the victims, the burglars had worn gloves; at any rate they hadn't left any prints, according to what the lab had turned up. Aside from the general descriptions—young, fairly big, both white men, one possibly with blond hair—there was just nothing. And by what they had turned up, that pair had got away with something like four thousand bucks in cash, and the rest of the loot might have yielded another five hundred from pawnshops; none of that was identifiable. In spite of the attempted education on the subject of crime, few people kept records of serial numbers. And as far as the cash went—people like that, who would only go out shopping for the necessary supplies a couple of times a month, and didn't have the kind of bank balances which afforded free checking, would tend to take cash for the pension checks. Roughly, the only thing those people had had in common was that they were all ordinary middle-class people, neither very rich nor totally poor, and they'd all been elderly. It was just a big mystery, and Katz didn't like it worth a damn. For one thing, as he said to Varallo, most of the victims had been fairly frail old people, scared and shaken up if not actually harmed physically; it was on the cards that one of these nights one of the victims might have a heart attack or a stroke, and the mystery would get elevated into a homicide. And there wasn't one damn thing to be done about it, no suspects to question, nowhere to look.

Katz put the reports back together, centered on the blotter on his desk, and sat staring into space, thinking.

The LAPD man was Lieutenant Daley of central Narco, and he sat in the other chair in O'Connor's little office puffing at a disreputable-looking briar pipe. He was a paunchy man in his fifties, with a cynical mouth and hard gray eyes.

"Well, that's the word we've got, O'Connor, and informants have handed us some useful info before. There's supposed to be a big drop somewhere in this town, a big wholesale stash—H, coke—a supply dump for a ring of dealers all over the county."

"And why the hell pick Glendale?"

"Oh, we heard that too." Daley looked amused. "Anybody knows the Glendale cops are cream puffs, the cleanest town around and you're not used to dealing with those tough pros— of any kind."

O'Connor flung himself back and the desk chair creaked under his bulk. He barked a savage laugh. "Is that a goddamned fact? With the stuff all over every school ground and sellers on every block south of Broadway—and the rate up here, damn the kind, the way it is everywhere—"

"Still not as dirty as my beat or a lot of others in a lot of places. Compared to some towns, Glendale's nice and clean, even when the rate's up. I can see it might be an ideal place for a supply dump. And if the informant's got it straight, it's a couple of the big boys behind it."

"Syndicate bosses," said O'Connor.

"That's just what. The word is this is where it goes when it comes in, either over the border or from farther off."

"The picture's changed in the last ten years or so, sure, a lot coming in from the East Coast." Absently O'Connor reached up to adjust his shoulder holster where the .357 magnum bulged. "You can't search every semi crossing the California border, and private planes—cars— Hell and damnation."

Daley struck another match to keep the pipe lit. They didn't need to discuss that in detail. One of the problems with the foolish powder was that it didn't take up much space, and in terms of street profit, a million bucks' worth could be stashed under the front seat of a truck or in a suitcase in a private car. "If it's Syndicate," said O'Connor, "it'll be ninety per cent H and coke."

Daley said placidly, "More like a hundred per cent. That's where the profit is." They both knew that too. The marijuana came in over the border, or got grown and processed locally; one of the latest curious problems to law enforcement were the anonymous gangs using national forests for pot plantations. The PCP got manufactured locally; that, and the various pills—amphetamines and the rest—was petty stuff in money terms, and the Syndicate largely let it alone.

"Any lead as to how it's distributed?"

"Nary a lead. Educated guess, a few fairly high up henchmen move it in batches to pass on to the wholesale dealers. We've just got one name. Sardo. The informant isn't parting with his source, but that made us sit up. My God, do we know Sardo, and a hell of a lot of good it does us. A lot of Narco cops here and back east know Tony Sardo. He's been in the racket for thirty years, but he's been clean since he did a one-to-three for dealing in New York nearly twenty-five years back. Nobody's ever got anything on him since. He's probably fairly high up in the Syndicate by now. He owns a very high-class restaurant in West Hollywood, the Polynesian Inn, that's the front. Even if we had any reason to go over his books, there'd be nothing showing. He won't be handling stuff himself, he just makes the deals by remote control. This is supposed to be Sardo's supply dump."

"And just what the hell do you suggest we do about it?" asked O'Connor.

"Just passing information on," said Daley, puffing. "Possibly we might hear something else, but the informant's nervous and

I can't say I blame him. Those boys aren't safe to meddle with, no way."

"So you give us just a handful of nothing. Just a big supply drop somewhere in town, and it could be anywhere from one of the new two-hundred-grand condos to a furniture warehouse on San Fernando Road!"

"I know, I know," said Daley. "It's never an easy job. We just thought you'd like to know."

"Thanks so much," said O'Connor.

"Well, we're poking around as best we can, and if we get anything else, I'll let you know." O'Connor just growled at him. Daley knocked out his pipe in the ashtray and went out, and O'Connor was still sitting there thinking about that when there was a diffident tap on the open office door. He looked up.

"Excuse me, Lieutenant." It was one of the uniformed Traffic men, McLeon. He came in and loomed over O'Connor, a good deal taller if no broader, and said, "We all got briefed by the watch commander a while ago about these joints—if we came across any, you're supposed to get 'em."

O'Connor sat up. "Show," he said tersely.

McLeon produced a paper bag and upended it on the desk. "I got chased down to a junior high school on Glendale Avenue just now. The principal called in. Holy God, riding a squad may not be the easiest job in the world, but sure as hell I'd rather be doing that than trying to ride herd on the punk kids. The principal had just had a bunch of them up for fighting on the school ground, and he'd confiscated these off one of 'em. The minute I laid eyes on them, I spotted them for the kind of joints Lieutenant Gates was talking about. Damn unusual joints. So I brought them in."

O'Connor looked at them without pleasure. There were three of them, and that made an even dozen he'd seen in the last four months. As joints—marijuana cigarettes—they were unusual, if that was the word for it. "Thanks very much," he said to McLeon. "Did you get the name of the kid who had them?"

"Sure. Dave McKinney, he's in ninth grade. A big fat kid about fifteen. None of the kids would utter, just called me a couple of names."

"That figures," said O'Connor sourly. "OK, McLeon, thanks."

The Traffic man went out, and he opened the bottom drawer of his desk, brought out a box with the other nine joints in it, and laid them alongside the new collection. The average joint was sleazily made, the thin brown paper carelessly stuck together, loose-packed marijuana showing at both ends. At first glance these might be ordinary machine-made cigarettes, neat and firm and close filled. They looked like ordinary nonfilter cigarettes, but the filling was pot all right. And if his sense of smell was accurate, it was high-grade marijuana, undiluted. They were a very superior product indeed, and probably retailed at double the usual street price. And a fifteen-year-old—well, that was nothing new or surprising even if it was damned discouraging when you wondered what the next generation was coming to.

He contemplated them glumly, got up, resettled his tie, and took all twelve of them downstairs to the Juvenile office. He found Detective Mary Champion bent over her typewriter with a cigarette in the corner of her mouth. It was Ben Guernsey's day off; she was alone in the office. She was a rather hard-bitten-looking dark woman in her late forties, with over twenty years of police experience behind her.

"And what can we do for you, O'Connor?" She removed the cigarette and looked up at him.

O'Connor laid out the peculiar joints on her desk, and she said interestedly, "Some more of these. Funny."

"Not so very," said O'Connor. "The latest three are off another kid—ninth grader, Dave McKinney."

"And you want me or Ben to have a heart-to-heart talk with him and his pals and try to find out where he got them."

"You read my mind."

"Where do we find him?" He told her the school. "Well, see what we can do, but those other kids just weren't talking. And the rest of those, I seem to remember, you came by at different places. Some of them from Hoover High, wasn't it?"

"That's right. There were a couple of them on a kid from Hoover grabbed for purse snatching, and three on a suspect on a heist we brought in for questioning, and the rest on a kid from Glendale High picked up in a hot car. Nobody would say where they came from—claimed they bought them from a guy on the street, didn't know his name, never saw him before."

"A likely story," said Mary. "It'd be interesting to know where they do come from, O'Connor. Such pretty little things. All I can say is, somebody at least is giving value for the price. Well, we'll let you know if we get anything out of the kid."

Delia got in a little late on Wednesday morning. It was cold and gray again but no more rain in sight. O'Connor and Varallo were the sole occupants of the detective office; it was Lew Wallace's day off, and evidently everybody else was out on the legwork.

"Anything new go down yesterday?" she asked, hanging up her coat.

Varallo told her about the suicide-murders and she grimaced. "All the sister kept saying was, it was all on account of Christmas, it preyed on his mind that he couldn't buy any Christmas presents for the family. He'd had a good job at an assembly plant in the valley but they started laying off because of the recession. The wife had been hunting a job too, but no luck. They were behind on the rent and there wasn't much food in the place. The sister had come over to stay with the little boy while the wife applied for another job—he was supposed to be out looking too. He had an old Ford, but it'd died on him, and I guess that was another last straw."

"The things we see," said Delia. "Nothing showed up on any of the heists, I suppose."

"You suppose right. That Polanski wouldn't even look at any mug shots, said it would be a waste of time. He did tell us that one of them looked a lot like Gil Gonzales." Delia laughed. "You feeling all right?"

"Just fine," said Delia, smiling at them. Curiously it was true. As far as she had felt for nearly two and a half years, Alex had already been gone; last week had just put the final touch to it; and he would be all right somewhere. She had kept busy yesterday on the various household chores, and she'd had a long talk with Laura on the phone. Laura had been a good friend. On the whole, she'd decided, looking at it objectively, she had a lot to be thankful for. She would put the house up for sale as soon as

Alex's will was through probate; it was a simple will and wouldn't take long, the lawyer had said. Spring, she thought vaguely; in any case it wasn't the time to try to sell a house; nobody went looking at houses in winter, this near Christmas. And if it was an old house, it was a substantial one in a good residential area and ought to bring a good price. She wondered about investments; probably the lawyer would have some ideas. And then a bright new little apartment somewhere—there were new apartment buildings going up here every month—a place easier to keep house in, a place easier to live in alone.

Varallo smiled back at her, running a hand through his crest of tawny blond hair. "You missed the dog," he said.

O'Connor had one hip perched on the corner of Leo Boswell's desk. "Funniest little mutt you ever saw, named Rosie." He was telling her about that when Rex Burt wandered in with a manila envelope in one hand.

"Joe not in?"

"I don't know where he is," said Varallo. "Out on some more legwork on that weird pair of burglars, probably—that one's really driving him up the wall."

"Well, we did some good on that 459 yesterday," said Burt. "Picked up a couple of dandy latents on the windowsill. I ran them through R. and I. downtown, and there he was. A small-timer, he's done little piddling spells in for petty stuff, including a couple of other burglaries. He's still on parole from the facility at San Luis. I've got his package here."

"Very gratifying," said Varallo. "You boys sometimes do earn your keep." Burt left the envelope on Katz's desk and wandered out.

A couple of minutes later a couple appeared and hesitated in the doorway. "Is this the detective office?" asked the man. "The sergeant downstairs said to come up—"

Varallo stood up. "Yes, sir, that's right. What can we do for you?"

They were a rather distinguished-looking couple, both probably in their late forties. He was tall and spare, balding, with a fringe of gray-brown hair and pleasantly rugged features, intelligent dark eyes. He was well tailored in a navy suit, white shirt, and tie, and carried a tan raincoat over one arm. She was short and slim, once very pretty and still attractive, with brown hair and discreet makeup; she was smartly dressed in a black pant-suit and a tailored wool coat. They came farther into the office, and Varallo pulled up a couple of chairs to his desk. "I'm Sergeant Varallo—Lieutenant O'Connor, Detective Riordan. Sit down, won't you? What can we do for you?"

The woman took a quick breath. "It seems so impossible," she said, "but we decided the police had better hear about it. Because it's so queer. And Bob says that is blood—and we thought—"

"Can we have your name, please?"

"Oh, I'm sorry—yes, of course—"

The man said in a heavy baritone, "Myrick. Robert and Carla Myrick. I'm with Locke, Powers and Shepherd downtown." That was a well-known old firm of stockbrokers. "It's Carla's aunt. Aunt Lila. Mrs. Lila Finch."

"Yes?" said Varallo.

"Well, it's just impossible," said Carla Myrick, "but she's disappeared. She's—just gone. And nobody seems to know where. Nobody's seen her in days, by what we—and she lives such a quiet life, she doesn't go out much, she can't drive at night, and she never goes away anywhere. If she'd been going somewhere, she'd have told us—and when I couldn't get her on the phone, we thought we'd better check—I mean, she's quite well and active, but she is sixty-eight and she could have had a fall—" Her pretty face was distressed. "I've got a key to the house—"

"Excuse me," said Delia, "does your aunt live alone?"

"Yes, she's a widow, Uncle Louis died ten years ago, they never had any children. She's my mother's youngest sister. And we went to the house—it's on Kenneth Road, they bought it nearly thirty years ago, it's too big for her but she just kept it on, she always said it'd been home so long she wouldn't feel right in an apartment—"

"Is she pretty well off, Mrs. Myrick?" asked Varallo.

"Oh yes—Uncle Louis was in real estate and construction, she owns a couple of apartment houses—"

Myrick cleared his throat. "I look after most of her estate, Sergeant. There's a parcel of blue-chip stock, she's got an income of around sixty thousand a year after taxes. She's a very sensible old lady, quite a good business head. In a way, that's why we got worried—she's not one to go off half cocked."

"We went to the house," his wife broke in agitatedly, "and she'd gone. And her mink coat's gone and all her jewelry—the car's in the garage, and I don't think any of her clothes are missing except the coat. But we've called all her friends, and nobody's seen her or talked to her since Thanksgiving—it was all because we went up to Linda's—"

"Now, Carla," he said.

"When did you see her last?" asked Delia.

"Well, that's just it! We usually had her for Thanksgiving, of course, but this year Linda asked us all up there—our daughter, she and Gordon live in Fresno—and we hadn't seen the baby since last spring—and Aunt Lila was going with us, but at the last minute she decided not to, she said she didn't feel up to the trip, she thought she was coming down with the flu and she'd just stay home and be quiet. She looked just her usual self, and we took her out to dinner—that was the Tuesday before Thanksgiving—and we drove up to Fresno the next day. She'd said maybe she'd be with Mrs. Adair on Thanksgiving, that's an old friend of hers, she's a widow too. And we decided to stay on a few days and then as long as we were there we went on over to Santa Cruz to see Bob's sister—I tried to call Aunt Lila from Linda's but she didn't answer, and I really didn't worry too much about it then. I said she doesn't drive at night but some of her friends do, and they go out sometimes—to dinner or the theater—not very often but sometimes. I wrote her a note and told her we wouldn't be back right away—"

"It was in the mailbox," said Myrick.

"And a lot of other mail—well, not a lot but some—I suppose early Christmas cards—I mean more than just a day's delivery—and I called Mrs. Adair and Mrs. Irving, and they'd tried to call her too, they both thought she'd decided to go up to Linda's with us, they weren't worried—"

Myrick said, "Carla. Better put in some dates. They're about her closest friends. They'd both talked to her a couple of days before Thanksgiving, not since. She usually went out to her bridge club on Thursday—"

"But with everybody so busy, getting ready for Christmas—

all of the women have families—they weren't going to meet in December. We called four or five of her friends, and nobody had seen her or talked to her since before Thanksgiving—they all thought she'd gone with us—and when we looked through the house—oh, it's just impossible!" said Carla Myrick a little wildly. "But she lives by such a set routine—she isn't out at night once in a blue moon, and when we found the mink and her jewelry missing—we didn't get home until Monday, and of course I called her right away—"

Myrick said half apologetically, "It sounds damned melodramatic, I know, but I think she could have been kidnapped and murdered. There's some blood on the workbench in the garage —I think it's blood."

Delia looked at Varallo. "Does she have any servants, Mrs. Myrick?"

"Just a cleaning woman—once a week—and the gardener. I don't know much about them—but she'd just fired the cleaning woman, that was the day after we saw her last—she called me that Wednesday—she said she was going to get one of these monthly maintenance services, a lot more efficient. It was a Mexican woman she'd had, but she said she wasn't very satisfactory—and it all sounds just like Bob says, melodramatic—but where is she? Nobody's seen her or talked to her for two weeks —we thought we'd better report it to you, because—well, *where is she?*"

"I don't know what you might think," said Myrick. "She lives such an orderly routine life—and she's a very active, sensible old lady, not one to fall for a confidence game—but my God, that house—I'd talked to her about leaving the jewelry at home, but she wouldn't listen, she said there were good locks and what was the use of jewelry shut up in a safety deposit vault? She had quite a lot of it—her husband believed in diamonds as investment—and I don't know, but word could have got around. It sounds melodramatic, but we thought—well, what do you think?"

Varallo looked at Delia, at O'Connor. "I think," he said, "we'd better have a look at that house. And the alleged bloodstains."

"Good," said Myrick simply.

CHAPTER 3

Varallo and Delia followed the Myricks up to the house on Kenneth Road. It had developed that the Myricks lived in Pasadena. Kenneth Road, north in the city, was a very old but very good residential area, and Lila Finch's house was typical, a solid big tan stucco house on a wide corner lot. Myrick unlocked the front door, and they went into a square entry hall; a large, dim living room was on the left, dining room to the right. There were heavy gold drapes pulled over the living room windows. "That's another thing," said Mrs. Myrick, "the drapes closed— she always opens them first thing in the morning. And you can see nothing's been dusted in a couple of weeks, and she's a good housekeeper, a little fussy about that, she doesn't let things go. You can tell there hasn't been anybody here for a couple of weeks at least."

In silence they looked at the rooms; the furniture was old and solid, the heavy traditional style of twenty or thirty years ago. The large kitchen was neat, no used dishes on the counter tops or in the sink; a small electric oven and a blender stood together on one side of the sink. The refrigerator, next to the service porch door, hummed softly. Delia asked, "Did you look in the refrigerator?"

"There's not much in it, but she doesn't cook much for herself, she uses a lot of frozen things, it's easier for a person alone."

The upright freezer in the service porch was moderately full of frozen entrées, TV dinners, vegetables, concentrated fruit juices, a couple of cakes; a good supply.

They went down the central hall to the master bedroom. There were three bedrooms, the other two furnished adequately. Lila Finch had occupied the biggest one at the front. There was a big walk-in closet. The bed was a four-poster wal-

nut double bed, neatly made up with a quilted royal blue bed-
spread. Delia turned that back; the bed was neatly made up
with clean-looking sheets. Varallo was contemplating the closet,
and she went to look. The closet was full of clothes, neatly hung
up, many of the dresses and suits protected by plastic covers;
there were a couple of long evening gowns. "There's just the
mink coat gone," said Carla Myrick, "and all the jewelry."

"Where did she keep it?" asked Varallo.

"In a couple of big jewelry chests, one on the dressing table
and one on the bureau." The dressing table was bare except for
an old-fashioned linen runner and a couple of half-empty bottles of cologne. Varallo pulled open the top drawer, using his
pen on the knob; it held a box of face powder, a used powder
puff, jars of foundation cream, tubes of lipstick.

"Would you know if all her handbags are here? Was that the
one she'd been using lately?" There was a padded bench at the
foot of the bed and the only thing on it a black leather handbag
standing open.

"I don't know, she had a lot of bags, but probably so, when it's
there." The bag held a few odds and ends, a little cosmetic case
with a powder puff and lipstick in it, a used handkerchief; no
wallet. "Yes, of course she carries a billfold sort of thing, with
her driver's license and a double purse for cash and slots for
credit cards—"

"Which ones did she have?"

"Just Visa, and she has an account at Buffums'."

"Might be a good idea to notify them the cards might have
been stolen."

"Does she have any luggage, Mrs. Myrick?" asked Delia.
"Where might it be?"

Carla Myrick said blankly, "Heavens, I don't think so. They
never traveled, Uncle Louis didn't like to be away from home.
They never went anywhere."

"She had a lot of clothes," said Varallo.

"Yes, she's a very smart dresser, she likes nice clothes, she
always looks nice—she's not a recluse, you know, I didn't mean
that, she goes out a good deal, alone and with her friends,
shopping and so on—the library, she likes to read, and sometimes she goes to a movie in the afternoon—"

They went on looking, and in the front hall closet found a single ancient battered suitcase, empty. "These bloodstains," said Varallo.

They trooped out to the detached double garage at the rear of the house. There was a padlock hanging on the big door, and Myrick said, "It was locked, incidentally. We have a key for that too. But she's a careful woman, always keeps the garage locked if she won't be using the car, and at night."

Varallo swung the door up. At the left side of the garage was a six-year-old white four-door Cadillac, looking clean and well kept. Myrick led them over to the workbench built along the other side of the garage and pointed silently. The workbench was rough unpainted wood and held a few not unusual odds and ends: a new-looking can of wax remover; a topless carton holding a few tools—screwdrivers, wrench, pliers; a package of new lightbulbs. And at the front end of it, there were several sizable splotches staining the rough wood, a dark reddish brown. "Yes," said Varallo, "it looks as though somebody did a little bleeding here all right."

"I thought so," said Myrick uneasily.

"Well, it all looks suggestive," said Varallo. "It certainly doesn't seem that she went away somewhere voluntarily, was planning to be away from home. There are no signs of any struggle, any violence, but there wouldn't necessarily be."

"And the house on the corner," said Delia, "the neighbors probably didn't see or hear anything."

Mrs. Myrick said, "There wasn't anybody home there yesterday—Aunt Lila knew them, of course, just casually—a Mr. and Mrs. Mallory, they've lived here nearly as long as she had, their children are all grown and they're pretty social, they're out a lot —he's a lawyer."

The house next door was a two-story brick place. They found Mrs. Mallory home, a svelte blonde by request, much made up, and she listened avidly to the little story and said, "My good heavens alive, you think something's happened to her? Such a nice woman, not that we know her very well—I can't get over it, right next door—" But she couldn't tell them anything useful. She thought the last time she'd noticed Mrs. Finch was the day before Thanksgiving, she'd seen her drive away from the house and that was just chance, she wouldn't usually notice, the drive being on the side street, but she'd just been leaving herself. She hadn't noticed any cars parked in front of the house, but Mrs. Finch didn't often have company. And she and her husband were out a lot, they didn't pay much attention to neighbors coming and going. She thought the gardener had been there on the regular day, she'd seen his truck, he came on Wednesdays: not the same gardener they had. She hadn't noticed anything unusual next door; sometimes she wouldn't see Mrs. Finch for a couple of weeks. "You think something's happened to her? But if she had an accident, she'd have been identified—is her car there?"

Varallo dodged any questions; they went back to the corner house. The house on the other side, on the side street, was separated from the Finch house by the backyard and garage, and the Myricks said those neighbors probably wouldn't know anything, they were a younger couple named Johnson who both worked, were away all day.

"I don't know what you can do about this," said Myrick.

"A few things we can do," said Varallo. "We'll get the lab to do some testing and tell us if that's blood in the garage, and go over the house for any strange prints. You'll both have left some, and we'll take yours for comparison. We'd like the names and addresses of her friends—did she have an address book?"

"Probably, in the desk or somewhere," said Mrs. Myrick. "We can tell you some names."

"Did she have a regular doctor?" asked Delia.

"Yes, Dr. Spaulding here in town."

"Well," said Varallo, "let's go back to the station and get your prints, and we'll keep the keys to the house."

"Surely, any way we can help you, sir," said Myrick. "I don't like to think what could have happened, but it looks as if something happened to her, doesn't it?"

"It surely does, Mr. Myrick. We'll see what we can find out."

Katz and Poor had been out talking to those burglary victims again, but it had been a waste of time; there just wasn't any link showing. They broke for lunch and went back to the station, and Katz found the manila envelope Burt had left on his desk.

He had a look at the contents and said pleasedly, "Well, now and then we do get a break. Of course, few of them are very smart. Here's Mrs. Kohler's burglar, and he's just what we might have expected, John. Rodolfo Calderon, a middling little pedigree with us and L.A.—burglary, car theft, possession—he's still on parole from his latest time in. He left some nice prints on the windowsill. He lives down on Elk Street—let's go see if he's home."

The address was a ramshackle old duplex in that rundown section of town, and a fat young woman with a distinct mustache opened the door. She had a heavy accent on the English. She looked at the badges and stepped back reluctantly. *Sí*, Rodolfo was here—they came to arrest him again maybe—she shrugged. "He no good to me anyway, out of work all the time, just lay around. No-good bum, I should have listened to Mama when she said don't marry up with."

Calderon was in his early thirties, a stocky, dark fellow with a straggly beard. He looked at them sullenly and wouldn't say much. They ferried him back to the station and sat him down in an interrogation room and talked to him for a little while. Not long, because there was the evidence placing him at the scene, and they didn't need a confession. He was stupid, but not stupid enough that he didn't realize that, and finally he said resignedly, "So OK, I pulled that damned job, and for a lousy forty bucks the hock shop give me. The P.A. officer, he got me a job in a gas station but the guy fired me, and the old lady always at me for bread—so you send me back to the joint, big deal, at least I get away from her yappin' at me all the time, and they feed you pretty good."

Poor started the machinery for the warrant on him and Katz booked him into the jail. He had a dollar and forty cents on him, and six marijuana cigarettes wrapped in a dirty handkerchief.

The weather bureau was never altogether reliable; the forecast had been no rain, but about one o'clock it began to drizzle again. There were more people on the street than usual, people out Christmas shopping; these days Brand Boulevard wasn't the general shopping area it had once been. The big stores and specialty shops were now concentrated over in the big shop-

ping plaza, the Galleria, on Central. But there were people out
on Brand too, still shops and business offices along there. At two
forty-five, with the rain coming down harder, there were people on both sides of the street—a couple of women waiting for a
bus at the northwest corner of Broadway and Brand, people
waiting for traffic lights to change at all four corners of the
intersection—so there were witnesses to describe what happened. The lights were red on Brand, the Don't Walk signs up
on Broadway, and three people were crossing the street on
Brand, when a car coming north ran the light at high speed.
Two of the pedestrians had got to the center dividing strip; the
car hit the third pedestrian without braking and roared on up
Brand weaving slightly, leaving the pedestrian sprawled against
the center strip. A few people ran up shouting, more people just
stopped and stared, and somebody called the cops from the
bookstore on the corner.

When Patrolman Neil Tracy got there about ten minutes
later, he called in for an ambulance before he got out of the
squad, and then went to look at the body. And it was a body all
right; a woman, and she was dead, very dead. It looked as if the
car had caught her squarely and run right over her; her head
and legs were smashed, oozing blood and brain tissue. Feeling
rather sick, though he'd seen a lot of bad accidents, Tracy
looked around in the street; there was a crushed green umbrella, a canvas shopping bag spilling paper packages in the
rain, and about fifteen feet away a handbag. He picked that up.
Half a dozen people were crowding up, trying to talk to him. "I
saw the whole thing, she was crossing the street, she had her
umbrella up, she couldn't have had any warning at all, it was
terrible—" "I can tell you about the car, Officer, I was right at
the corner, it was a big car, I think it was a Caddy—" "He didn't
even try to brake, must have been doing about fifty, he went
right on up Brand—my God, she's dead, isn't she, just an awful
thing—" "It was a Lincoln, and it hit the divider strip after it
knocked her down, maybe damaged a front wheel, I heard it hit
but he never even tried to brake—my God, is she dead?"

The handbag was a shabby brown leather bag, good-sized.
There was a wallet in it, and the wallet held a driver's license

made out to Jean Hoffman, with an address on Spencer Street in town.

The ambulance came, and the attendants got out and looked. "Jesus," said one of them, "she never knew what hit her. You want the morgue wagon, not us." Tracy said he knew that. He also wanted Homicide detectives. He turned to the crowd and began to collect names and addresses. As usual, the witnesses didn't all agree on the story, but Tracy thought two of them, both men, sounded more certain and factual than the rest, who were all pretty excited. He scrawled names in his notebook. John Lindsay, Rossmoyne Avenue; Peter Babcock, Stocker Street. He took down all the other names.

"The detectives will want to talk to you, probably."

"Anytime," said Babcock. "That was just plain damn murder." Lindsay just nodded gravely.

It was raining harder and the body was getting soaked, the blood washed thinly into the street, and the packages and the shopping bag were sodden. Tracy put the handbag into the squad and picked up the shopping bag. As he did so, one of the packages came apart and spilled its contents onto the wet pavement—a big stuffed dog with a lolling pink tongue and a pink ribbon around its neck. The driver's license had said that Jean Hoffman was thirty-one. Tracy felt sick all over again.

The ambulance left and the morgue wagon came up. Even in the rain the crowd had stayed to stare, from all four corners of the intersection. But when the body was gone it was all over, and they started to drift away. Tracy got back in the squad, called in, and drove back to the station.

In the detective office upstairs, he handed over his notes, the handbag, and the shopping bag to Varallo, and told him and Delia Riordan about the scene, the witnesses. Nobody could say anything about the driver, man or woman—it had all happened so fast. Nobody had got even a partial plate number, of course. But according to the two witnesses, the two good ones, the car had hit the center divider pretty damned hard. It may have sustained some damage.

"And if we can spot it," said Varallo, "there may still be some blood on the front end somewhere."

"And there may not, in all this rain," said Delia.

"OK, Tracy, thanks, we're on it," said Varallo.

Tracy went back on tour, thinking of that poor damned woman—a young woman, maybe a husband and kids—and just before Christmas—

There were things that had to be done on one like that. Delia called the address on Spencer and got no answer, so she went up there and tried the house next door. There, she talked to a middle-aged woman who burst into tears at the news, gave her a little relevant information incoherently. Such a nice young couple, Roy Hoffman worked at Olson's Electric Service on Glendale Avenue, no, Jean didn't work, and there were two children and she'd probably have left them with her mother, she wasn't sure of the name but somewhere here in town.

Delia went up to Glendale Avenue and found Olson's Electric Service. Hoffman was there, just back from a service call, a tall, dark, good-looking fellow. She broke the news to him gently, another part of the thankless job. He couldn't seem to take it in; he kept repeating dazedly, "Jean's dead? You're saying Jean's dead?" Three or four other men rallied around. She explained about claiming the body. One of the other men said, "We'll take care of him, miss, thanks. God, what an awful thing to happen—" She did get the mother's name from him, Mrs. Marjorie Abernathy on Glenwood Road, so she went there next.

The mother was a sensible, practical woman and stayed in control, on account, Delia thought, of the children—two children, a boy about four and a girl about two. She asked Delia to call her husband at the real estate office where he worked.

When she got back to the station, it was nearly the end of shift, and Varallo hadn't reached any of the witnesses except Lindsay and Babcock, just ten minutes ago.

"You feel like doing a little overtime? I'll call Laura—you can come and take potluck with us."

"Fine," said Delia soberly. "What a dirty thing, Vic—those two kids, and her husband, and just before Christmas. Just a stupid, careless driver, maybe drunk—"

"And the odds are against catching up with him," said Varallo wryly, "but we have to try." He got on the phone to Laura.

They drove up to Hillcroft Road in Varallo's Ford, and they

didn't talk about the hit-run or any of the other office business to Laura and the children. Laura had dinner nearly ready; they had a drink beforehand, and Delia began to feel slightly more cheerful.

It had stopped raining when they started out again to talk to the two witnesses. Lindsay lived in this same section of town, a comfortable old house not far away from the Varallos'. He was an elderly, rather handsome man with a fine head of white hair, and it turned out that he was a retired army colonel. He introduced them to his pleasant, plump wife courteously. She said, "John's been telling me all about it—an awful thing. These drunk drivers—"

"I don't know anything about the driver," said Lindsay quickly. He had, he added, just come out of the bookstore on the northwest corner of Brand when the accident happened. "Accident," he said, and snorted. "It was murder, plain damn murder —inexcusable. The way the car was being handled, the driver could have been under the influence. But I'm familiar with cars, I'm used to observing carefully, and I don't lose my head easily. I can tell you about the car. It was a Lincoln Continental, I'd say about three or four years old, and it was light blue. It was doing about forty-five, entirely too fast for the middle of town, of course. I couldn't say anything about the driver, I'm afraid—I just saw the woman struck, and then the car was past the corner —yes, it rammed into the center divider, I heard it hit. But that's definite, a Lincoln Continental, light blue." He sounded very sure, and he was an intelligent, observant man.

Peter Babcock, at an apartment on Stocker, was much younger, a man in the early thirties with a pretty blond wife. He told them he'd been off work that day because he had an appointment with the doctor, he'd been coming down with the flu, and he still felt pretty damn rotten.

"But not rotten enough that I wasn't seeing straight—God, what a thing to see happen!" He'd been on the way back to his car in a lot on Maryland; the doctor's office was on Brand a block away. He'd been waiting for the light, on the same corner where Lindsay had been. "It was a big car, I'd have said a Caddy, but this other fellow said a Lincoln Continental and it could have been, all right—seems, looking back, it did have a little longer nose than a Caddy. And he's right, it was light blue —kind of what they call powder blue. I didn't get a glimpse of the driver, sorry—it all happened so fast—I happened to be looking down Brand, and the first thing I thought when I saw the car coming, he was speeding, and then it hit me, my God, he's not going to stop for the light—and then, bang, it hit that poor woman, she didn't have a chance, probably never saw the car, she had her head bent under the umbrella—God."

Those were probably the best witnesses. On the way back downtown Varallo said, "Write a report in the morning. We can go through the motions. Brief Traffic to alert all the garages—if the car did get some damage, he'll likely take it in for repair. And drunk or not, the driver knows he hit her. So, not just garages in town—Eagle Rock, Pasadena, Atwater. In case he tries to be cute."

"Yes," said Delia. "Vic, what do we think about the Finch woman?"

Varallo rubbed his handsome straight nose. "Well, it's a funny one. Offbeat. But the way she's described, nice quiet woman living a routine life, and the way that house looked—just vanishing away without warning—hell, she could have been abducted. The most available valuables missing and her wallet—it doesn't look so good."

"By what the Myricks found out, the key date seems to be Thanksgiving or the day after. Nobody seems to have seen her since. And she didn't—by the house—leave voluntarily. I wonder why she fired the cleaning woman. We'd better find her and ask."

"They thought her name was Espinosa. There should be an address book somewhere." They were letting the lab look there first. "But, for God's sake, if she was kidnapped—"

"Get a warrant to look at her bank account," said Delia rather sleepily, "in case she's been forced to write any big checks. The only point to an abduction. But I don't think that's what happened at all. I've got a sort of gut feeling about it, after seeing that house. I think she's been murdered."

"For the mink coat and the diamonds? But what would be the point of spiriting the body away?"

"I don't know, but quite a lot of ignorant people have the idea that we can't prove murder without a body. I just don't feel it was a—a planned thing, Vic. Suppose she had an argument with somebody—somebody like the cleaning woman, or the gardener—a casual workman of some kind—and the fact that the blood was in the garage rather suggests somebody like that—"

"We're waiting for the lab to say if it is human blood."

"Yes. But suppose. And he's suddenly stuck with a body— knocked her down and fractured her skull or something. You can see somebody like that, in a way, deciding to get rid of the body, and ransacking the house for valuables as an afterthought."

"And how the hell would he get rid of the body in the middle of town?"

"I couldn't have a guess. But something's happened to the woman."

"There I'll go along with you. See what the lab can tell us." He dropped her off in the parking lot where she'd left her car. "I'll come in early to brief Traffic about those garages." The Traffic day shift would be getting briefed about any daily business just before eight o'clock.

Patrolman Michael Whalen had just gone on swing shift, and he liked it a lot better than the midnight-to-eight tour. You were apt to get more business, accidents and drunks and brawls, but it wasn't as boring as riding a squad alone all night with only the radio for company. He came in at three-forty, sat through the briefing by the watch commander, and took over the gassed-up squad at four. His beat was South Central through town. It was dark by five, but at least it had stopped raining; it had turned a lot colder. He cruised around the assigned streets, listening absently to the radio. Other cars got sent to an accident on Glenoaks, a heist on Glendale Avenue, and an unknown disturbance on Verdugo Road. He didn't get a call until just after six, when he was sent to a third-rate bar on South Central to deal with a fight. It wasn't much of a thing: two half-drunk Latins pulling the knives. Neither of them was hurt much, and the sight of the uniform calmed them down. The bartender said they both lived in the neighborhood, so they wouldn't be endangering the citizens by driving; he persuaded them to go home. He cruised around the beat again. The big shopping plaza, the Galleria, was in his territory; everything was open at night now for the Christmas shoppers, and there was quite a lot of traffic coming and going. At seven o'clock he called in a Code Seven and stopped at a coffee shop on Central for dinner. He was back on the beat by seven forty-five, but he didn't get another call until eight-fifteen.

It was an address on Milford Street, and that was one of the blocks of old frame and stucco single houses, a very modest residential area but nothing like a slum: Glendale didn't have any real slums. The house was an old California bungalow dating from the twenties, and it had a neat green lawn and some rose bushes in front. The porch light was on; he went up on the porch and rang the bell. The woman who opened the door was about forty-five, stout and plain faced, and she talked to him through the screen door. She said her name was Ida Fischer.

"I'm Mrs. Doty's housekeeper, this is her house, she's in a wheelchair with the arthritis and I take care of her, sure I live here too. The reason I called you, we've been wondering about Mrs. Phelps next door. Mrs. Doty noticed it this morning when she was in the living room watching TV—the front door's open, and it looked funny—it's been so cold, and Mrs. Phelps is an old lady, she feels the cold. But we didn't think to look again—Mrs. Doty always takes a nap in the afternoon and I was busy in the kitchen—until just a while ago when we went into the front room to watch TV, and you can see the door is still open, because there's a light in her living room, and we thought maybe she's had a fall or been taken sick and somebody ought to check and see."

"You didn't go over to look?" asked Whalen.

"I'm scared to death of that dog of hers, it's a snappy little thing and I'm scared of dogs anyway—"

"All right, ma'am, I'll check on it."

The house next door was a square stucco place, with just a strip of lawn in front. As he came up on the tiny porch, he could see the front door was wide open, light shining beyond; there wasn't any screen door. He sang out, "Hello, there, this is the police, is anything wrong here?" He got no answer, and went into a long, narrow combination living-dining room. It was furnished comfortably enough with shabby old furniture; there was a black and white TV in one corner, two doors leading to the rear of the house. He tried the one at the far end of the room and looked around a small, neat kitchen. There was a hall leading out of that, and he looked into a very small rear bedroom sparsely furnished with a single bed and dresser. There were lights on all over the house. He went on down to a second bedroom, and on that threshold he stopped and said, "Jesus Christ!"

Nobody would ever be afraid of Mrs. Phelps's dog again. The dog, a nondescript tan terrier, was beaten into a bloody pulp at one side of the double bed. The old woman was another bloody pulp at the foot of the bed, and nearly on top of her body was the bloody smashed body of a small black cat. "Holy God," said Whalen, and backed into the living room. He knew better than to touch anything. He went out to the squad and called into the station, and then he went back next door.

"Is she all right?" asked Ida Fischer.

"No, ma'am," said Whalen bluntly. "I'm afraid she's dead. It's a good thing you called in."

"Oh, my goodness—we were afraid something had happened —was it a heart attack? That's awful—"

"Do you know if she had any relatives?"

"Yes, there's a daughter, I think her name's Bergman, she comes to take her shopping, I don't know where she lives but maybe Mrs. Doty would remember her first name—"

Whalen waited for the night watch detectives, and they told him he could go back on tour. Sobered by that bloody scene, he started cruising again, and five minutes later he got chased down to a heist at an all-night pharmacy on Los Feliz. The pharmacist was scared and mad.

"Comes in here with a gun like a cannon and cleans out the register, he got about a hundred bucks, and all the pills—he was after the amphetamines, all the rest of the stuff these junkies use —sure I can tell you what he looked like, he was maybe six feet and medium blond, stringy long hair and a bad case of acne— maybe eighteen or so—I'm alone in the place after nine, and am I going to argue with a gun like a cannon? Goddamn it, this is the second time we've been held up in six months—"

He'd have to talk to the detectives tomorrow, thought Whalen. Right now the night watch was busy.

That was the first call the night watch had had. It was Rhys's night off, and Hunter and Harvey both went out on it. At the first sight of that bedroom, Harvey said, "Jesus. What have we got here, a homicidal maniac?"

"That's what it might look like. My God in heaven," said Hunter. "What a thing. And there's not much for us to do but preserve the scene for the lab." There might be some useful scientific evidence in that room, the rest of the house. Harvey used the radio in the squad to call in; there'd be somebody there up to midnight. They sent the squad back on tour, and talked to the neighbors Whalen had already seen. All they could tell them was her name, Mrs. Amanda Phelps, and that she was a widow, lived alone, had a married daughter, she was about sixty-five, and she hadn't gone out much.

"Do you know who lives in the house on the other side?"

"Sure, Mr. Lowder," said the Fischer woman. The other woman just sat in her wheelchair looking pale and shaken. "But you shouldn't go bothering him, he wouldn't know anything. The poor man just lost his wife last month, it was cancer, it hit him pretty hard. Mrs. Phelps was a friend of hers, he'll be sorry." They were still thinking it was a heart attack or a stroke.

Back on the street, Hunter said, "If that door was open all day —and by the look of that blood—it could have happened last night."

"The autopsy will say," said Harvey. The mobile lab van pulled up behind his car, and Ray Taggart got out of it. He looked at the scene and said, "My God, the jobs we get handed. The return of Jack the Ripper. I suppose this one gets the works." He started to take pictures first, and they left him to it and called the morgue wagon from the van radio. The morgue wagon could have the body after Taggart had got the photographs.

It was still only nine-thirty; they tried the house on the other side of the Phelps place and talked briefly to an Adam Lowder. He was an elderly man, and he looked to be in bad shape, sneezing and coughing with a heavy cold. He just looked dazed, hearing about Mrs. Phelps. He said helplessly, "I'm sorry, I don't know anything about it—I've been in bed all day, the doctor gave me some pills—"

"Hell," said Hunter after they left. "Unless the lab turns something, it could be just the anonymous thing."

"At least it wasn't the two offbeat burglars. Katz has been saying they'll kill somebody, but not like that."

"God, no," said Hunter. "I'll tell you what it could be though, Jim. That much blood lost, the mindless violence, it could have been the doped-up junkie just doing what comes naturally."

"Which is a thought."

Taggart was still busy. The morgue wagon arrived, and they started back to the station. Let the day watch take it from here.

That was the first thing there to be looked at on Thursday morning, and Varallo swore. There had already been another heist yesterday late afternoon, and after the homicide had showed up, there had been two more heists and the victims were due in to make statements. But having read Harvey's report, he and Delia went out for a first look; this would be one to work into the ground. They left Gonzales to take the statements on the heists.

Taggart had got photographs last night, but there would still be a lot of lab work to do in that house. They found Burt and Thomsen busy doing it, dusting surfaces.

"And we're not nearly finished with that place on Kenneth Road," said Burt. "A house that size—no, damn it, I can't tell you anything about that yet, we picked up the hell of a lot of latents but who's to say they're not mostly the Finch woman's? We haven't got hers to compare, damn it. This damn job is like women's work, always something else coming along. And what the hell are we supposed to do with these poor damn animals, bury them in the backyard?" The bodies of the cat and dog were still there, an unpleasant, bloody sight, stiffened in death.

"You'd better call Animal Regulation." They looked around the house without disturbing the lab men. It was impossible to say whether the house had been burglarized; there weren't the usual signs—drawers dumped out and cupboards left open—but that might not say anything here. There weren't many clothes in the bedroom closet. An old handbag on a chair in the living room contained a wallet with about seven dollars in cash in it. But the same thought had occurred to both of them that had hit Hunter last night: the mindless violence could mean one of the junkies operating at random.

Burt came out of the bedroom and said more amiably, "Well, we may have a shortcut. You notice that X left us the weapons."

"I didn't look that close. What?"

Burt displayed them: a heavy hammer with its handle wrapped with black tape, and a two-foot length of rough two-by-four. Both were liberally bloodstained; even the hammer was dark with dried blood. "The two-by-four wouldn't take prints," said Burt, "but there are some dandy clear latents on the hammer."

"Beautiful," said Varallo. "Now if they just happen to be in somebody's records—"

"Don't be a spoilsport. We'll find out," said Burt.

There was an address book beside the telephone in the living room. The Doty woman next door had given Harvey the daughter's name last night, Miriam Bergman, and there was a number labeled Miriam. "So you can go and break the news," said Varallo. "I'd better get back and help Gil out with the heist victims."

The phone had been printed. Delia called the listed number and talked briefly with Miriam Bergman; her address was in Hollywood, Las Palmas Avenue. She drove over there through heavy traffic. It was an old apartment, and Miriam Bergman matched it, a plump woman in the forties with blond hair needing a new dye job, a discouraged-looking woman in a shabby cotton housecoat.

"We'd like you to look through the house and say if anything's missing," said Delia.

"I just can't believe it," said Miriam Bergman blankly. She'd been crying; she looked ill and shaken, with red-rimmed eyes and trembling hands. "When you said on the phone—Mother murdered! Just killed—it doesn't seem anything that can happen—I talked to her on Tuesday, I usually call her every couple of days—she was just fine—I always went to take her to market on Saturdays, you know—she'd got along pretty OK since Dad died a couple of years ago, I took her shopping and all—" She was talking numbly, at random. "You were lucky to get me, usually I'd be at work, I work at Louise's Dress Shop on Sunset, only I've had this awful cold, I've been just rotten for a couple of days, couldn't go to work—I'm divorced, see—but I just can't believe this, Mother—"

"By what we can deduce so far, it probably happened on Tuesday night," said Delia. "Of course, we aren't sure yet. Do you think your mother would have opened the door to a stranger after dark?"

Miriam Bergman blew her nose. "I don't know," she said drearily. "She wasn't suspicious of people—I'd tried to tell her, be careful about keeping the doors locked—but I don't think she realized about the awful crime rate—I guess she could have. The screen door broke a couple of months ago, she wanted to get a new one—I mean, you keep the screen door locked, it's some protection—but they're expensive—and she always said Tippy would scare a prowler or burglar—oh, my God!" She uttered a dry sob. "That funny, fat little old dog—oh, my God, it's just terrible to think of them getting killed too—she just doted on them, Tippy and Sammy the cat—she'd had them for years, she fussed over them, she loved them so much—and they were getting old, Tippy was thirteen, he was going deaf, and she'd had Sammy before she got him—I just can't believe anything like this could happen—"

CHAPTER 4

Two of the heist victims had been willing to look at mug shots, hadn't made any in Glendale's records, so Gonzales had taken them down to R. and I. at Central LAPD. By the descriptions, none of the heisters were the two Latins who had been hitting the jewelry stores. By midafternoon, the lab called to say they were finished at the Phelps house, and Delia called Miriam Bergman to ask if she felt up to looking around there. She said miserably she guessed so, she'd come over.

Delia met her there, and she looked through the house and said there wasn't anything missing as far as she could see. Her mother hadn't had much, was just getting by on Social Security. She'd owned the house—"They finished paying for it about twenty years ago, it's about all she had to leave me." She looked at all the dried blood in the bedroom and shivered. "Oh, my God, all this—" The bodies of the cat and dog had been taken away by the Animal Regulation Department. "I suppose I'll have to hire somebody to clean it all up—" Delia told her about the mandatory autopsy, about claiming the body. She just nodded. "I expect her keys are somewhere, I'd better lock up if you people are finished here. But who'd have wanted to kill Mother? She was just an old lady living alone, no money or anything valuable to steal—it doesn't make sense."

"She hadn't had any trouble, with teenagers on the block or— did she hire anybody to cut the lawn, do any work?"

Mrs. Bergman shook her head. "She used to have a kid down the next block mow the lawn, but the last six months she just let it go, it cost too much." Only the recent rains would have turned the remaining grass green. "It doesn't make sense. Nobody would have anything against her, she never hurt anybody in her life—just an old lady living alone—and I guess they didn't steal anything, there wasn't much to steal."

It didn't make much sense. Even if it had been the hopped-up juvenile, looking for loot to support a habit, he wouldn't have missed even the little cash in the handbag; the house hadn't been ransacked. "Nobody would have any reason to kill her," said Miriam Bergman, "and Tippy and Sammy."

It looked as if Amanda Phelps had opened the door to somebody, and possibly been attacked at once, tried to get away, and been struck down in the bedroom. By the homicidal maniac? They did occur, and this house could have been picked just at random. But there were the good latent prints on that hammer.

Delia got back to the station at four-thirty and found the detective office empty except for Leo Boswell and O'Connor, who was sitting at Varallo's desk talking to Mary Champion. O'Connor said, "Both your new heist victims made some mug shots, Vic and Gil are out chasing them up. We heard something about that messy kill."

"Very messy," said Delia, "but there were prints on the weapon, we'll see if they show anywhere."

"Well," said Mary, "I'm sorry we couldn't be of any more help, Charles—this McKinney kid, as I said, is a typical little snot-nose, isn't telling cops anything. He got those joints from a guy on the street, an older guy—which might mean anything from eighteen to fifty—the guy just said did he want to buy, and he did. He was mad as hell at the principal for stealing them, said they were the best joints he'd ever got, and they were two bucks each but worth it."

"Understatement," said O'Connor. The average joint sold for about a dollar apiece, but the superior products would be worth the double price—if you were in the market for joints. "Damn it, a fifteen-year-old, and that section of town—they get the money somewhere—"

"Dipping into Mama's purse," said Mary cynically. "But that's about it. And we've got a nasty little case of a twelve-year-old seduced by her older brother, I'd better get back to it. The doctor thinks she might be pregnant. And we like to think mankind has made any progress in this enlightened century?

My God." She stabbed out her cigarette in the ashtray and went out.

A messenger from Communications came in with a couple of manila envelopes addressed to O'Connor and Varallo. O'Connor passed that one to Delia and looked at the contents of the other one. "Autopsy on that OD—nothing in it, he was full of H and liquor. Progress! Goddamned fool kid killing himself at eighteen."

The other one was the autopsy report on the Fullers, the suicide-murders, and there was nothing in that either, just the expectable.

Delia had finished the first report on Amanda Phelps, and they sat there talking desultorily until Varallo and Gonzales came in looking tired and glum. Varallo said, "Get out of my chair, Charles. This has been a waste of a whole damn day."

"You didn't do any good?" asked Boswell.

"Between them those victims picked three mug shots, and two of them had the right pedigrees for the heist. We located both of them and they've got alibis."

Gonzales yawned and sat back tiredly. "One of them was getting married yesterday afternoon, all correctly witnessed by the priest of St. Anthony's and about forty guests, and the other one's in the hospital with a leg in traction."

"The way the job goes sometimes," said Boswell philosophically.

"Thank God tomorrow's my day off," said Varallo. The phone rang and he picked it up. "Sergeant Varallo."

It was Burt at the other end. "I just thought I'd let you know, we'll get a report to you sometime, but that house on Kenneth Road—that was human blood on the workbench, type O. It's been there awhile."

"So thanks. It would be the commonest type." He passed that on.

Delia said thoughtfully, "Get hold of Lila Finch's doctor, he'd know her blood type. If it's type O, it says something, Vic. And I'd like to talk to the cleaning woman and the gardener. We haven't talked to any of her friends yet."

"Damn it, it just broke," said Varallo, "and there are only twenty-four hours in a day. And this Phelps thing—"

"Who's Finch?" asked O'Connor. Delia told him, and he was interested. "That's a damn offbeat one, and nowhere much to go on it. What the hell could have happened to the woman?"

"I think she's dead," said Delia.

"I'm inclined to think so too. But the body—"

"I suppose we'd better have a look at her bank account," said Varallo. "We haven't got a description of the jewelry worth a damn. The Myricks could just say diamond rings, an emerald necklace, it's nothing to put on the pawnbrokers' list."

"Unless a body turns up, it may stay up in the air," said O'Connor. He heaved himself up, resettled his crooked tie. "I'm going home." It was nearly the end of shift and no time to do any more on anything. It was already dark. Delia emptied the ashtray into the waste basket and got up with them.

Downstairs the maintenance crew had just arrived, several large men in tan jumpsuits. Two of them were mopping the tile floor in the lobby, a couple of others putting a new fluorescent strip light in the hall. They'd be busy cleaning up the whole station for the next six hours, as usual on Thursday nights. The night watch wouldn't be in for a while.

Friday was Varallo's day off. It was the month for cutting back all his roses, but he didn't feel much like all that work; maybe he'd get to it next week. Laura took Ginevra to school, took Johnny with her to the market. Varallo wandered around the backyard and did a little pruning, but it was cold and damp outside and presently he settled down with one of Laura's library books. Gideon Algernon Cadwallader got up in his lap and curled up comfortably; he was a big, heavy cat, but Varallo put up with him resignedly.

Delia got in on the stroke of eight on Friday morning and called the lab, but didn't raise anybody for fifteen minutes, when she got Thomsen. He said, "Oh, those prints. I was just going to call you. The prints on that hammer from the Phelps house—we ran them through records here and downtown and they didn't show, so we sent them to the Feds." The FBI had millions of prints on file, and not all of them known criminals.

"We should get a kickback in a day or so, sometimes they're backlogged."

"Fine," said Delia. "The Kenneth Road house—did you come across an address book?"

"Oh yeah," said Thomsen, "there was one on the desk in the living room. We can take it most of the prints we picked up there belong to the Finch woman, and there were some others, we're sorting out the relatives' prints now, see if any of the rest don't match. But aside from that blood, the place is clean, no sign of any violence."

"I know, but it still looks as if something happened there."

She left Gonzales starting out to hunt for possible suspects on the heists, and that was the slow way to go at it but often the only way, finding men in Records with the suggestive pedigrees and hauling them in to question. She drove up to the house on Kenneth Road; she had the keys, and let herself in. The house was gloomy and depressing and very cold. She found the address book in the top drawer in the little French desk in the living room, and leafed through it. They had the names of most of Lila Finch's closest friends from the Myricks, and she recognized those; to save time, talk to those women on the phone, but not this early. Mrs. Finch had been a methodical woman, her handwriting neat and plain. There was a J. Espinosa, listed with a parenthetical addition, *cleaning,* and later on a Galetti, *gardener,* addresses as well as phone numbers—one in Eagle Rock, one in town. She decided the gardener might start work early, but she might catch the cleaning woman at home, and started for Eagle Rock.

There was more traffic than usual—Christmas shoppers. As she came into Eagle Rock, she caught the light at Colorado and Ellenwood, and a black and white squad stopped beside her in the left lane. She thought about Jean Hoffman. Varallo would have talked to the watch commanders here and other places; and the men cruising in the squads all around here, in Pasadena and Atwater and other places, would have been alerting all the garages where a car might be left for major or minor repair, the garages asked to call in about any light blue Lincoln Continental with front-end damage. But the car needn't have sustained enough damage to need professional repair; they might never catch up to that car and driver. In any case, by now there'd be no way to know if the driver had been drunk, if he had been. There were some very stiff new penalties in for drunk drivers now.

She found the address, a little old frame house on a narrow back street, and found Mrs. Josefina Espinosa at home. She was a thin, dark, middle-aged woman without much accent on her English, and she answered questions readily, volubly. "Sure I worked for Mis' Finch, and I tell you, I'm still feeling good and mad about it—you said you're police, why are police asking about that? Don't tell me she went to you about it?" Her dark eyes flashed. "That'd be the limit! I'll have something to say about that—what do you mean, she's gone?" Delia explained economically. "Well, I don't know nothing about that, she never said nothing to me about going away anyplace, but the last time I saw her was the day before Thanksgiving, I always went to her Wednesdays, all day, did the floors and mirrors and sometimes the windows, and cleaned the stove, and all like that. That was the day she fired me, why, I'd been working for Mis' Finch for six, seven years and she always seemed like a nice lady, first I was surprised and then I got mad, and I said if that was the way she felt, good-bye—"

"What reason did she give?" asked Delia.

"Well, that's just it, she had the nerve to say that Manuel stole some money out of her purse, and he never would, he's a good boy—that's my boy, he's eighteen and in his last year of high school, sometimes he did some of the heavy work for her, earn some extra money, and just the week before, he'd been there on Saturday, stripped the wax off the kitchen floor and put on new —he took my car, I don't take jobs on Saturdays—and she never said nothing to him then, it wasn't until the next Wednesday I was there she said that, she said I'd always been satisfactory but after she found Manuel stole some money she didn't feel right about having me there anymore—calling us thieves, it was an insult!—I was good and mad—she said she'd get one of these regular companies to come in, and she paid me what she owed me—and I was so mad I just walked out, didn't stay to do any work. And I don't know a thing about her going away anyplace."

Delia asked more questions but that was about it. Mrs. Espinosa was a widow, and Manuel her only son. Getting back in the car, Delia reflected that that sounded nice and straightforward, but there could be more to it. Particularly to Manuel. Mrs. Espinosa might be an honest woman, but Manuel—an eighteen-year-old—in her comings and goings in that house, Mrs. Espinosa would have noticed the mink coat, the jewelry, and probably mentioned it to Manuel. And he, or he and a like-minded pal, could have been sniffing around there intending to try a break-in and been caught by Lila Finch. Delia still felt, if Lila Finch was dead, it had been a spur-of-the-minute thing, not intended or planned. But the body—so if it had happened that way, Manuel or somebody else, why cart away the body? Unless something about the body could give away the killer, and she couldn't imagine what that could have been.

She went back to Glendale, thinking, and started to get on the phone to Lila Finch's friends. They had probably told the Myricks all they knew, but something fresh might emerge when they heard the police suspected abduction or homicide. And ask for the warrant to look at her bank account.

About three o'clock that afternoon Rex Burt straightened from the microscope at the workbench in the lab and said to Thomsen, "Well, for what it's worth, it looks like a Colt .32." One of the heisters, at a bar on Verdugo Road, had taken a shot at the bartender when he'd been slow opening the register, and the slug had hit the wall. Burt had gone out to dig it out this morning, and had just now got around to looking at it. "If the detectives ever pick up the gun, we can match it." He filed it away in a labeled box, stashed it with other evidence. They hadn't had any kickback from the Feds on those prints; well, sometimes they didn't get on it right away.

It was hot in the station, the heat turned up by the main thermostat in response to the outside temperature. He lit a cigarette and went out of the lab to the back door, opened it for a breath of the fresh cold air. As he stepped outside, something dodged past his legs and ran through the door—a dog. "Hey," said Burt. It was a little black hairy dog, and it ran down the hall and started up the stairs. Burt ran after it. "Hey, you, come back here—what are you doing here?" He didn't catch up to the dog until it got upstairs and into the detective office.

O'Connor was sitting at Varallo's desk talking to Boswell, Poor typing a report across the office; Delia Riordan was on the phone. The dog ran over to O'Connor, wagging its stubby tail. "The damn thing got in when I opened the back door," said Burt.

"Well, by God, it's Rosie again," said O'Connor. The dog seemed pleased to see him, and he bent to pat her. "Damn it, she's got out of that woman's yard again. What the hell was her name?" He looked at the dog's collar. "Beal—somebody said she lives just a couple of blocks away up the street. Damnation, we'd better call her."

"Cute little dog," said Boswell. "Funny it should show up here again."

Delia put the phone down and came to make friends with the dog, who smiled at her and licked her hand. "Why did you say she was funny-looking? She's sweet."

"Well, fifty-seven varieties."

"Oh, you and that high-class hound of yours. What's the number? I'll call the woman." The dog sat down beside her desk and scratched one ear.

Burt said, "Well, if you know where it belongs—" and went back downstairs.

Delia got on the phone and listened to it ring six times before she got an answer. "Mrs. Beal?" She explained about the dog, and Mrs. Beal was vexed.

"Heavens, somebody must have left the gate open again— I'm so sorry—I'll be right over to get her. I've only had her six weeks or so, she was my father's dog, and it's the queerest thing how she runs to the police station—"

"Well, if you would come and get her," said Delia politely. "There's a leash law, and it's not safe for her to run loose."

"No, of course not, I'll be right over." She showed up fifteen minutes later. Rosie had curled up contentedly at O'Connor's feet and went to her a little reluctantly. Gonzales had just come in towing a hulking, very black fellow, and Delia was on the phone again; Mrs. Beal apologized all over again, clipped on Rosie's lead, and led her out.

"Somebody like to sit in on the questioning?" asked Gonzales, and O'Connor followed him and his captive down to an interrogation room.

The suspect looked like a promising possible for one of the heists; he had the right record for it, and the people at the bar had described the heister as a big Negro. O'Connor and Gonzales asked questions, and he glowered at them and wouldn't say much except that he didn't know a damn thing about it, he didn't have no gun, he'd never been near that bar. They could hold him for twenty-four hours without arrest; O'Connor stashed him in the jail and Gonzales got on the phone to that bar. It was four-thirty then.

The bartender said, "Oh hell. Trade'll be heavy the next three hours, I can't get away."

"Tomorrow morning," suggested Gonzales. "You said you'd recognize him, we just want you to take a look."

"Oh hell. All right, I'll be in sometime in the morning."

Saturday was Gonzales' day off; he left a note for Varallo just in case everybody else forgot to mention it.

Poor sat back from his typewriter and said disgustedly, "People. You'd think that they'd have some respect for their own property."

"New burglary, I take it," said Gonzales. It was Katz's day off.

"My God," said Poor. "Great big house up on Olmstead, crammed with loot—the householder's an architect, you'd think an architect of all people would know something about security—nice dead-bolt locks on three outside doors, and a sliding glass door off the kitchen with just a flimsy catch. So they're surprised and mad as hell when they come back from an evening out and find they've had a burglary. And the loot, my God—two fur coats, a lot of good jewelry, big color TV, a combination stereo—"

"More than one man, to move that—they probably had a pickup."

"And the neighbors can't tell us anything, of course—couple on one side out too, and the people on the other side watching TV. All the windows shut, naturally, a cold night. I had Thomsen up there all morning dusting the place, but no bets they left any prints, it was a pro job." The burglary rate was way up, and it wasn't too often they could catch up with the burglars. In most cases there just weren't any leads to follow; it was a dead end. Poor slumped back in his chair and lit a cigarette. "Not another damn thing to do on it but file the report, see if the lab turns anything, but I won't hold my breath. Any of you doing any good on anything?"

"Not much," said Gonzales. It was too late to go out hunting for more possible suspects. They still had four more to locate, culled from Records; but let Varallo and Forbes do the legwork on that tomorrow. Delia was sitting back smoking with her eyes shut. "Have you turned up anything interesting on the Finch woman?" O'Connor had just come back and sat down again at Varallo's desk.

"Not really," said Delia. "The gardener hasn't been home all day, naturally—we'll probably have to catch him on Sunday. I've been talking to all her friends for a couple of hours, and it just continues to look—suggestive. The last one to see her was a Mrs. Adair, and that was the day after Thanksgiving. She says Lila was just her usual self, didn't mention any plans for going anywhere, any trouble or arguments with anybody. She's the only one who knew Lila hadn't gone up north with the Myricks. Everybody else thought she'd changed her mind and gone with them. All these women know each other, and ordinarily they'd have been talking on the phone oftener, seeing each other, but in December, with everybody busy planning for Christmas, some of them expecting company—her bridge club wasn't meeting this month, the last time they met was the week before Thanksgiving. The last one who spoke to her on the phone was a Mrs. Haley—and that was the afternoon of the day after Thanksgiving. She sounded just like her usual self, no mention of any trouble except that she did tell her about the Espinosas, that she was going to have one of those bonded maintenance companies come to do the cleaning. A couple of the women had tried to call her since, just assumed she was out shopping or somewhere. By the way, I got hold of the doctor, and her blood type's O. He's terribly curious, I'll bet he's a detective-novel fan. She's a very active, healthy woman for her age—the last time he saw her was early October, she came in for a flu shot."

"I thought the reason she didn't go with the Myricks," said O'Connor, "was that she was getting the flu."

"Well, shots don't always take. And maybe it was just an excuse—maybe she just didn't want to go."

"Those Espinosas," said Gonzales. "The kid Manuel. But hell, Delia, the possibilities are wide open. Just the way Myrick said, word can get around about a woman living alone, and that house in a good area, the possible loot. She could have come home from somewhere and surprised somebody starting to break in—anybody. I will say, some punk kid like that would likely just cut and run, if he'd killed her without meaning to, and the body'd have been there. Why the hell should anybody take the body off, if there was a body? The pro burglars wouldn't do that, no reason to. It's not so easy to get rid of a body, for God's sake, and why bother?"

Delia said placidly, "Just what I said to Vic, Gil. The only reason I can think of was to hide the fact that there was a murder. A lot of people think we can't prove murder without a corpse."

"But where the hell would you hide a body in the middle of a metropolitan area?" asked Gonzales reasonably. "I know, it happens—now and again a corpse comes to light buried under a house or in a lonely section of Griffith Park or some place, but not very often. And if it was broad daylight—"

"Which," said O'Connor suddenly, "we don't know, damn it." He'd been sitting listening in silence, smoking. "And I think I've just had one very damn interesting idea about that. Damn what time it was—just off the top of my mind, so she didn't drive at night, but sometimes she went out with people who did. Anybody with sense leaves lights on at night when they're gone, you might ask—some people don't. But damn what time it was, whether a break-in artist thought she wasn't home and she surprised him—"

"There'd have been some signs of a struggle," said Delia. "She was a strong, active woman."

O'Connor ran a hand through his curly black hair. "Damn it, it doesn't matter. She could have come home in the middle of the afternoon and found him prowling around the garage, and the fact that that's where the blood is makes that look more likely. And without any intention he found himself stuck with a body. All right. You haven't found her keys, have you?"

"No, keys and billfold both missing," said Delia.

"So all right. He had her keys and bag. And he thought if there wasn't a body to be found, there couldn't be a homicide charge. Figure it. He went away and came back after dark—if it wasn't dark then—and he went through the house at his leisure and collected the portable valuables. Left her rifled bag in the bedroom. He'd have a car. It'd be dark on that side street. The body was in the garage. Was she a big woman?"

"Middling," said Delia. "Five-five and slender."

"All right, he gets the body in his car and he drives down to the Wash and dumps her in." They sat up and stared at him. "No damn trouble at all, it wouldn't take him two minutes. Stop on one of the bridges, and after midnight not a soul around to notice."

"My God in heaven," said Gonzales, "that's one I never thought of—"

"And we should have!" said Delia. "Of course there'd be nothing to it—and ordinarily it'd have been spotted right away, but when we've had all this rain—" They looked at each other, thinking about that.

The Wash, that ugly necessary thing, snaked through the center of town from the foothills, following the original bed of the Los Angeles River. Ten months of the year its concrete canyon was dry and empty, but in torrential rains it might carry twenty feet of water traveling at high speed, sometimes boulders from the hills.

"My God, where would a body end up?" said Gonzales.

"I think we'd have to ask the city engineers about that one," said O'Connor dryly. "It goes underground somewhere out around Studio City, I think, but eventually it runs right down to the coast. She might have ended up out in the Pacific."

Delia was looking excited. "We'd better find out—if that's so, the body could have been picked up by the Harbor Patrol—"

"I wish you luck on contacting any city employees over the weekend," said O'Connor. "Damnation, if that's so, what the hell are a few more days? Even if the body ever was picked up,

maybe after a week under water, not enough left of it to iden-
tify, and it won't be still stashed away in anybody's morgue."

"But it's somewhere to go," said Gonzales. "I think you just
had an inspiration."

"So do I," said Delia.

With the weekend coming up, business might be on the rise.
Rhys and Hunter came in a little early; it was Harvey's night off.
Most of the business, of course, would belong to Traffic—the
accidents, the brawls, the drunks. Rhys had the radio on, turned
to police frequency; it made a low, monotonous background to
their idle conversation while they waited for a possible call. Just
after they came in there was a pile-up on the Ventura Freeway
involving five cars and a truck, but that was Highway Patrol
business, nothing for Glendale.

At nine-ten, Communications sent up word of a heist pulled
at a supermarket on Glenoaks, just at closing time. They went
out to hear about it. There had only been three or four customers in, none of them near the checkout counter where the
heister had showed the gun; they hadn't noticed what was going on at all. The checkout clerk was a young flighty blonde
about to have hysterics, and she couldn't give them any description except that it had been a lone man, fairly big, and white.
She didn't have any idea how much he'd got; the register tape
would tell them. By the time she'd started screaming and the
manager came from the back, the heister was out the nearest
door. Maybe tomorrow when she'd calmed down she'd remember more, but this looked like another anonymous one they'd
never close the file on.

They got back to the station at ten o'clock, and Rhys had
started to type the report when they got another call. This time
it was the pair of offbeat burglars again. The victim was a Mrs.
Ada Nolan, at a single house on Western Avenue. She was probably in her seventies, a fat old lady with gray hair in steel curlers,
and she was scared and indignant.

"They called me by name, and they said police, and a prowler
in the yard and they wanted to use the phone—I was just going
to bed—and I could see one had a uniform on, I had the chain on
the door—and you've got to help the police—" It had gone just

like all the rest, the stocking masks, the knife, one of them looting the house. Here they'd just taken cash, about sixty dollars out of her handbag. She was a widow, lived alone, and had a married son living in Sherman Oaks. They called him. She was too shaken up to describe the uniform except to say that it was brown. Which might sound like an army uniform, but they didn't put much stock in that. A regular army man might not be above burglary, but he wouldn't be such a fool as to commit it in uniform.

When the son got there they went back to the station, and Rhys called Katz at home to break the news that they had another.

Katz just sounded resigned. "Sixteen!" he said. "Sixteen in four weeks, and just no handle at all. I suppose she had some jewelry and they passed it up?"

"Well, yes," said Rhys. "She looks a little better off than some of the rest of them. After they left she went to look, but the only thing they'd taken was the cash."

"My God," said Katz. "And they knew her name. How the hell do they know? These people are all strangers to each other, there's no link among them, who in hell could know all of them by name?"

"Occasionally we get the real mystery," said Rhys.

Katz uttered a rude word. "I could damn well do without this one!"

On Saturday morning Delia was talking about O'Connor's inspiration to Varallo and Jeff Forbes when the bartender came in to look at the suspect.

Forbes took him over to the jail, and he took one look at the hulking big Negro and said, "Nah, that's not him. The holdup guy was about as black but not as big, and he had a lot bigger Afro hairdo, sticking out, you know what I mean. He's not the guy." Forbes let the suspect loose and he went in a hurry.

Back in the detective office, Varallo was having no luck trying to contact the city engineers' office. He said to Delia, "Have to leave it till Monday. After this much time another couple of days won't make much difference."

"But it could be the answer, Vic."

"Yes, now and then Charles has a bright idea," said Varallo. "Where is he, by the way?"

Katz looked up from reading a report. "He just got in, five minutes before you, when we had word there's a gang rumble about to erupt somewhere down back of Memorial Hospital. He took Boswell and Wallace with him."

"The Guerreros and Eldorados mixing it up again. Satan finding work for idle hands." Those were the two biggest gangs in the area, responsible for a lot of the petty crime—and some other kinds. "They'll be fetching some of them in for possession if nothing else, some of those boys have taken to dealing lately."

"The upcoming generation," said Katz. "Brave new world. I just hope our boys don't get knifed."

"Not with that equalizer Charles packs. Well, we'd better go out looking for these possibles. My God, this weather—if it keeps on like this, it'll set a record for a wet winter." It was drizzling again. He and Forbes collected their raincoats and went out.

Delia sat thinking about Lila Finch. Why none of them had thought of the Wash—it wasn't a thing that happened too often, the attempted concealment of a body, and usually it was a difficult and dangerous thing. But that would have been so easy —no muss, no fuss. Tilt the body over a bridge and let the spate of rainwater do the rest. And if so, the body was probably long gone.

She tried calling the gardener, Galetti, again presently, and this time got his wife. She said he'd probably be home about three, no, he wasn't working, couldn't do any work in the rain, he'd taken the kids to see his mother. Delia wasn't thinking seriously about the gardener now; she was more inclined to think about the casual or pro burglar marking the Finch house as worth tackling, and Lila Finch somehow surprising him. But better talk to the gardener anyway. You never knew where a lead would show up.

She got the checkout clerk half an hour later, from the market heisted last night. After talking to her for ten minutes, she was feeling exasperated with this specimen of her sex; the girl was an idiot. She might be capable of ringing up the pounds of coffee and TV dinners on the computerized register, but when any common sense was being handed around she hadn't been there. She was a thin girl about twenty-five, with shallow china blue eyes and a shrill voice.

"Honest," she said, "I was just so scared, I couldn't see straight —all I saw was that awful gun, I'm scared of guns, I just couldn't say what he looked like—I told the other cops last night—yeah, he was a white man, but I just couldn't say how old or what size or anything—all I saw was the gun, and honest, I was shaking so I could hardly get the money out to give him, and he was nearly over at the door before I had the strength to yell—what do you mean, look at pictures? You think you've got his picture? I wouldn't recognize a picture no way—it happened so fast—"

Delia got down a statement, which of course was worth nothing, and she signed it and went away. O'Connor, Boswell, and Wallace came back, looking wet and mad and discouraged. O'Connor said, "I do get so tired of the stupid damned little punks." They had booked six of the gang members for possession, and of course they'd be let loose on nominal bail and get probation, right back on the streets to cause more trouble.

Katz and Poor had gone out on a new burglary call. Delia looked back over the reports on Finch and Phelps, and presently called the lab. They hadn't got the kickback from the Feds on those prints on the hammer. "They get backlogged," said Thomsen. "We'll hear."

At a quarter past twelve she started out for lunch; downstairs she looked into the Juvenile office to see if Mary could go with her, but she and Ben Guernsey were talking to a couple of citizens, so Delia went on alone to the little coffee shop down the block. It was still drizzling. She dawdled over a tuna sandwich and got back to the station at one o'clock. Poor was in, typing a report, and told her Varallo and Forbes were questioning a suspect.

This time she sat thinking about Amanda Phelps. The reasonless, savage violence. And probably quite random; that could have been any dopey in the city. But it smelled of lunacy, with the little cash untouched, the wanton violence, the weapons left at the scene. It was just a toss-up whether the Feds would have those prints.

Galetti, the gardener for Mrs. Finch, lived on Myrtle Avenue.

At two-thirty she was just on the point of leaving to go down there and talk to him. She went down to the women's restroom and powdered her nose, renewed her lipstick; she thought impersonally, looking in the mirror, that she didn't look quite thirty-two after all; that new beauty operator had done a good job on the newest casual cut. She went back to the communal office for her coat, and the phone was ringing on her desk. Automatically she picked it up and said her name.

Sergeant Leach from Communications sat on the desk on Saturdays when Bill Dick was off. "You've got a new homicide," he said.

Delia repressed an unladylike word. "Well, I'm the only one in. All right, I'm on it. Where?"

"The public library on Harvard," said Leach.

"The public *library?*" said Delia. "For heavens' sake. All right, I'm on the way."

CHAPTER 5

The public library in Glendale had been new ten years ago; it was a big square building nearly flush to the street, with a big public parking lot behind it. The squad was in a red No Parking strip at the curb. Delia parked behind it and went in the front door, which was off to the side. She'd never been here before, she used the branch of the Los Angeles Public Library nearest the house on Waverly Place. The Traffic man was Morris; he was over at the side of a large open room and advanced to meet her.

He said, "Not much scene to preserve—this is the damnedest thing I ever saw. Somebody getting killed in a library, it's damn queer."

"So what's the story?" asked Delia. The library was just a big open space, rather plush looking, carpeted thickly, with vast stacks of books at either end. The middle space was furnished with little oases of chairs and tables scattered here and there— comfortable, low, upholstered chairs. There was a large, square, four-sided counter at the opposite end of this area, with several women clustered in its center. Little groups of people stood well back toward the stacks of books, staring.

Morris said, "Well, I've just heard the gist of it. I gather they're pretty busy on Saturdays, a lot of people coming and going, and some people come in just to sit and read, not just take books out. The librarians are mostly behind that desk, checking books out and taking them in, and wouldn't pay much attention to the people just sitting around. So there's no saying how long the girl had been here, one of the librarians says she checked some books out for her about an hour ago, she thinks. Anyway, one of the employees here, a high school kid who just works here Saturdays, was hauling carts of books around putting them back on the shelves, and he happened to pass by pretty close to this chair and noticed that the girl looked funny, way he put it—sick or something—and he took a closer look and called one of the librarians. She's dead, and there's some blood—looks like she could have been stabbed."

"Right here?" said Delia.

"That's right. It's over here." He led her over to the side of the huge open room where tall windows streamed rain. There was a pair of low chairs, one upholstered in green, one in gold, about four feet apart, with a little table between them. In the green chair was slumped the body of a girl with dark hair. Delia looked at the scene appraisingly. "Not much blood," said Morris, "but you can see it."

The girl had slid sideways down across the low arm of the chair, and the dark hair had fallen over her face, but Delia could see that she was young—seventeen or eighteen—around there. She had on a tailored tan dress, and a tan raincoat was draped across the back of the chair. There was a small red stain of blood about the size of a half dollar on the left breast of the dress, and she was dead.

"Funny isn't the word," said Delia. There was a black leather clutch bag beside the girl on the seat of the chair, and an open book on her lap. Delia bent to look, and it was a book titled *Hauntings* by Norah Lofts. There were more books in a canvas shopping bag on the floor beside the chair. Another offbeat one, Delia thought, and an awkward place to do all that had to be done. She asked Morris to call the lab, and went over to the librarians huddled at the desk. There were four of them, two middle-aged and two fairly young. She introduced herself and asked, "Does anybody know who the girl is?"

One of the young ones said, "I think her name's Parker, she's one of our regulars, she's in here most Saturdays. I checked out some books for her about an hour ago, I hadn't noticed she was still here. There were people sitting around reading, and we were busy, people in and out. What happened to her?"

"We don't know yet. Who found her like this?"

A hoarse voice behind her said, "Me." It was a tall, lanky boy about eighteen, with sandy hair and a prominent Adam's apple. He was looking a little scared. "I was taking this cart of books over to nonfiction, put 'em back, and I happened to notice she

looked funny, I went and told Mrs. Dawson and she went to
look. She's—she's dead, isn't she? That's terrible, she's just a
young girl."

"Did you know her?"

"No, ma'am, I've seen her in here before, but I don't know
her name."

Delia looked around the place. There were about twenty
people here. Morris could stop any more from coming in, but it
was going to make an afternoon's work.

The librarians couldn't tell her much more. While she waited
for a lab man, she started getting names and addresses; all of
these people would have to be talked to, however briefly.

The lab man was Thomsen. He looked at the body and said
mildly, "Of all places."

"All places indeed," said Delia. "Print that handbag first, will
you?"

He dusted it and raised a few smudges on its smooth surface.
"It's all yours."

Delia opened it. Inside was a slim billfold, a powder puff,
lipstick, a little package of tissues. The billfold held three single
dollar bills and some change. The first plastic slot showed a
driver's license, just issued this year, for Nadine Parker, an
address on Randolph Street. There was also a filled-out ID card
—in case of emergency notify Mrs. Margaret Parker, the same
address.

"You want pictures?" asked Thomsen.

"Yes, we'd better." Delia started to talk to people and got
exactly nothing. Some of the library patrons were avidly interested, some annoyed at being detained, but none of them told
her anything relevant. They ranged from a young housewife
with a noisy baby to an elderly bald man clutching a copy of
Playboy, and none of them looked likely to have had anything
to do with eighteen-year-old Nadine Parker. None of them,
they said, had noticed the girl at all. Most of them had been at
the stacks picking out books; four of them, including the elderly
man, had been sitting reading, nowhere near the Parker girl. As
she finished talking to them, Delia let them go; at the front door
Morris had already turned away some people trying to get in.

There wasn't much for Thomsen to do here; he printed the

book in the girl's lap, took a few pictures, and he was finished. The morgue wagon came to collect the body at four o'clock. Delia went to talk to the librarians again. The girl had been dead for at least a little while before the boy, Larry Dodd, had noticed her; whoever had killed her might have left the library an hour before. The librarians couldn't tell her much; there had been people in and out since the library opened at nine that morning, and they only knew a few names, the regular patrons who came in fairly often. They were uncertain about times, which was understandable. It would be an automatic job, checking books in and out. This was another offbeat one. Delia let Morris go; it was past time for the Traffic shift to change, and he'd be due back at the station. She sighed. It seemed all she'd been doing lately was breaking the bad news to citizens.

She drove up to Randolph Street, a good residential area of North Glendale. It was a handsome Spanish house on a quiet block, and a worried-looking dark-haired woman answered the door. She looked at the badge, and she said, "Something's happened to Nadine—I've been worried—she should have been home two hours ago—I'd have gone down there myself but my husband's got my car, his is in the garage—oh, God, what's happened?"

Delia got her to sit down in the pleasantly furnished living room and told her. She just stared blankly; she hadn't expected anything as bad as this. "Dead?" she said. "You mean—killed? Somehow—at the library?"

"We don't know much about it yet, Mrs. Parker. And I don't like to bother you with questions at a time like this, but if you could just tell me a few things—when did she leave, was she going directly to the library? Was she driving?"

"No, she hasn't got a car, of course," said Mrs. Parker. "She'd have taken my car but my husband had to use it, he had some work to do at the office—he ought to be home anytime—she took the bus, she left just after lunch, she was just going to the library, she always goes to the library on Saturday. She's always been a bookworm. And it wasn't raining hard then, she didn't take an umbrella—she called me from the public phone there, that was about one-thirty, she said she'd wait awhile to see if the rain would let up—oh, God, Nadine dead—killed—but how could it be?" She was still too shocked to start crying. About then Parker came in, a nice-looking man with gray hair, shrugging out of a wet raincoat; and then she did start to cry. "Oh, Ralph—it's police—and Nadine—"

He held her automatically, stared at Delia over her head. "But that's just impossible," he said numbly. "Nadine's only eighteen, a good girl, she's starting college next year—she isn't wild like some kids, we've never had any worry with Nadine—how could she be killed?"

You had to give people time. Delia told him they would want formal identification of the body, tomorrow would do, told him where to come, said they'd want to talk to them both when they felt up to it. He nodded at her dumbly; he looked gray.

It was a quarter to six. Delia didn't go back to the station; she drove through heavy traffic and pouring rain through the Atwater section, got held up at Riverside Drive, and got home at six-forty to the gloomy big house. She shut the garage door and went in, went around turning on lights. Rather unprecedentedly she made herself a drink while she waited for the TV dinner to heat. Sitting in the big lonely living room, she thought back to when she'd used to come home to Alex and Steve, one of Alex's delectable concoctions waiting, and Alex eager to hear about the job, reliving his career in hers. She thought with a little dreary amusement that it was a good thing she wasn't married; between the job and Alex's interest in recipes, she'd never learned much about cooking. These days it was easier to depend on the TV dinners. She finished the drink and went to get that out of the oven.

Saturday night was apt to be busy, and the night watch got called out three times to heists at a pharmacy, an all-night gas station, and a dairy store. For once they were given good descriptions of the three separate heisters, and all the victims agreed to come in and look at mug shots, but on the gas station job that probably wouldn't be any use; the heister was described as a kid about seventeen, so he wouldn't be in Records. It would make all the more legwork for the day watch.

When they came to the end of the shift and started home, it had stopped raining.

Sunday morning was clear and very cold. It was O'Connor's day off, and as usual, he took Maisie the Afghan hound up into the hills above Glendale College for her weekly run. She bounced around, long legs flying, and would have gone on galloping for miles—she didn't get as much exercise as a big dog needed—but it was too cold to stay out long and O'Connor took her home about noon. As usual, he went down to the station just to keep an eye on things. Only Varallo was there. He said everybody else was out chasing heisters or waiting for the victims to make some mug shots, and another offbeat homicide had turned up yesterday afternoon—Delia was on that. O'Connor heard about it and said, "Of all the damn queer places for a homicide. At least it's stopped raining."

"And for how long, who knows?"

O'Connor grunted and trailed back to his office, and thirty seconds later uttered an outraged wail. "And just where the holy hell did this come from?"

Varallo went to investigate. In O'Connor's office, in the middle of his desk blotter, was a cat. It was a shorthaired gray tabby cat, and it looked at the men warily but made no move to run. "For God's sake," said Varallo, "where did you come from?"

"How the hell did it get in?" demanded O'Connor.

Varallo approached the desk and reached out a hand, and the cat let him stroke its head without moving, but the green eyes were watchful. He said, "At a guess, when the Traffic shift changed, either last night or this morning. The men all coming and going, leaving reports in the watch commander's office, she could have slipped in then. If it was midnight, it was still raining, and she'd be wet and cold—this morning, at least cold. Nice cat." The cat relaxed under his stroking hand and looked a little less wary.

"Cats!" said O'Connor.

"She's a stray, Charles. Either never had a home or somebody tossed her out. People will do it, thinking cats can fend for themselves, which they can't in a city."

"It's a five-hundred-buck fine to abandon an animal in this state," said O'Connor.

Varallo went on stroking the cat, who suddenly began to purr.

"I'm inclined to think somebody was nice to her once, she's not wild—used to people. But she hasn't had a home in a while, look how thin and scrawny she is."

"Thin?" said O'Connor.

Varallo grinned at him. "Except in the middle. Where the kittens are. I think she's due to have them any day."

"Oh, my God," said O'Connor. "We can't call the pound."

"Well, no." Pounds might be a necessary evil but they weren't sentimental about kittens. "She's a good cat, Charles—if she got in at midnight, she'd be soaking wet, but she'd cleaned herself up all slick."

"What the hell do we do about her?" asked O'Connor.

Varallo straightened up. He said thoughtfully, "Well, surely to God on a force this size, there'll be wives, sisters, mothers who might want a kitten. Maybe find a good home for Mama cat too. I can't take her home, Gideon would have a fit and move out. Tell you what, Charles. We can make a place for her here pending the kittens and put a notice on the bulletin board downstairs —we might find somebody to take her right away."

"In my office?"

"Well, it's out of the way and fairly quiet. Cats can be fussy creatures. No sweat, Charles. Get her a nice box and a litter tray and feed her up."

"My God," said O'Connor. "The things that happen around here—"

And Varallo had said airily, no sweat, but when he came to actualities it got a little complicated. He went downstairs and begged a carton from the lab; it had held chemical supplies and was a good size. He got a *Times* off the rack in the lobby and lined the carton with it, took it up to O'Connor's office and put it on the floor beside the file case, and gently lifted the cat into it. She got out again immediately but sniffed around it interestedly. Varallo went out to the parking lot and drove down to the nearest supermart. He bought a plastic litter tray and several packages of Kitty Litter. By the time he'd added some paper plates, a good many cans of cat food, and some dry Friskies, the cart was getting full. He got a quart of milk and as an afterthought a can opener. Back at the station, he had to make two trips upstairs, and put the litter tray on the other side of the file case and filled it with Kitty Litter. The cat promptly got in and used it, covering up after herself neatly. "One thing about cats," said Varallo. "They come already housebroken." He opened one of the cans and emptied the contents onto a paper plate.

"Look," said O'Connor, "my office—"

"Well, you're not really in it much, are you?" The cat was fastidiously investigating the plate, and began to eat the cat food appreciatively. "Good girl," said Varallo. "She'll settle down just fine." But he couldn't put the milk in a paper plate. He filched one of the glass ashtrays from the big office, washed it in the men's room, and poured some milk into it. The cat moved over to that. Then of course he was left with the rest of the milk. He took it downstairs to the lab and asked Burt to put it in the refrigerator there.

"You've got an ulcer?" asked Burt.

"No, a cat." Burt was intrigued, and went upstairs with him to see the cat. The cat had now got into the carton and was sitting on the *Times* washing her face.

"Well, I'll tell you," said Burt, "my mother likes cats, and she's just lost one she had for years. I'll bet she'd like one of the kittens, I'll ask her."

"Good," said Varallo. "You do that. It'll be a while before they can leave Mama, of course."

"Chasing me out of my own office," said O'Connor, but he squatted down to pat the cat. "She's sort of homely, but maybe if we fatten her up some—"

Varallo used the back of a report form to make a notice about the cat and expected kittens, and went down to pin it up on the bulletin board. The day watch commander, Gates, was just coming down the hall with a paper cup of coffee, and stopped to read the notice with interest. "Kittens," he said. "We might take one, my wife likes cats and so do I. When are they due?" Varallo explained that they weren't sure, but he could have a look at Mama cat in O'Connor's office. "My God," said Gates. "You've got her here?"

"Well, she picked out the place herself."

Ralph Parker had met Delia at the morgue and formally identified the body as his daughter Nadine. He was, of course, still numb and shocked. The morgue was in the basement of the Community Hospital, and she asked him to wait a minute while she looked into Dr. Goulding's office. He was there, tall and bald and genial as ever, and he said, "I just had a glance at that one. It looks as if she was stabbed. Tell you more about the knife when I've had a look inside. But my good God, that other corpse you handed us on Thursday—is there a homicidal maniac around? I just did that autopsy yesterday and the poor woman was battered to jelly—bones broken, skull caved in."

"He left some prints, we'll hope somebody knows him."

"And," said Goulding, making a face, "this damned hit-run. These goddamned irresponsible drivers. My God, she couldn't have been over thirty. I'll send up both reports. Oh, her skull was crushed and both legs broken."

Delia took Ralph Parker up to the big, quiet lobby of the hospital. They sat in a corner away from the admittal desk, and he lit a cigarette with trembling hands. "You know we have to ask some questions," said Delia. "Had your daughter had any trouble at school lately, can you think of anyone who might have wanted to harm her?"

"That's silly," he said. "No. She was a quiet, good girl, Miss Riordan. Not wild like some teenagers. She was an A student, she wanted to be a teacher—and try to write—she was going to start at UCLA next year, she'd have graduated from Hoover High in February."

"Did she have a boyfriend?"

"My wife and I have been talking, of course, and that's the only thing I can tell you, and that's silly too—just impossible. Nadine was a quiet girl, as I say—she wasn't much interested in going out a lot, she liked to read and she was a serious student, spent a lot of time on homework. She'd dated for the last couple of years, but not much, and it wasn't anything serious—no regular boyfriend. But the last few months, since the beginning of the new term, this one boy had been after her to go steady. Mark Schafer. Naturally she'd been a little—well, carried away —at first. He's a big name on the football team, quite an all-round athlete, and as you can imagine, he's sort of a hero to most of the kids."

"Yes?" said Delia. "Was there any trouble between them? Had they been going steady?"

"No, not really. Naturally Nadine was flattered, most of the girls in her class would be thrilled to pieces—as they'd say—to be given a rush by the big athletic star. But after she'd been out with him a few times, she told us he was just—how she put it—a nothing, when you got to know him. Like a lot of athletes, he's not much of a brain and he bored her. Nadine was a very bright girl, she was a great reader as I say, and she liked to talk about— oh, literature and art and authors, and music—she'd studied piano since she was six—and she found they just didn't have anything in common, you see. She'd turned him down for several dates lately, and he'd tried to argue about it—I guess he was really crazy about her—puppy love," and he sounded tired. "She was—she was a very pretty girl, you know." He'd been chain-smoking; his voice was dull.

"Do you think he might have been angry enough to want to hurt her?"

Parker sketched a negative gesture. "No, that's ridiculous. We'd met him, of course—he's just a sort of simple, big, good-looking kid, immature for his age, but good manners—just nothing much to him. He was probably disappointed and mad that she wouldn't go out with him again, but that's all there was to it. There wasn't anybody with any reason to hurt Nadine." He drew a painful breath. "Look, Miss Riordan, I know—about a lot of the teenagers these days. Even the ones from good families, well brought-up—the pressures they're under about sex and drugs—but you've got to believe me, Nadine wasn't one of them. We'd talked to her straight about these things. She was a —a good girl. Serious. Ambitious."

"Well, we'd like to talk to some of her friends," said Delia. Nadine Parker sounded like the nice girl he described, but even the nicest girls told their friends some things they didn't tell parents.

He nodded. "Surely. There's Sue Norman, they were all through school together. And Linda Barlow—Betty Cannon— Cindy White. They were about her closest friends. Yes, they're all in her class at Hoover High." Delia thanked him. "You'll let us know when we can—have her? I don't think we've taken it in yet—it isn't anything that could happen, Nadine killed."

They went out to the parking lot together; he got into his Chevy sedan and drove away. Delia went back to the station. There, of course, she heard about the cat, and went to look. The cat was curled up in the carton asleep, her gray and black tabby stripes shining and sleek. "She's a nice cat," said Varallo.

"To think of her picking Charles's office—" Delia chuckled. "I'd like a cat or a dog, but it wouldn't be fair to the animal when I'm away all day." And about then Forbes brought in one of the possibles on the pharmacy heist, and Varallo went to sit in on the questioning.

She hadn't finished the initial report on Nadine, and went back to that. It had been another gray, overcast day, and it was beginning to get dark by four-thirty when the phone rang on her desk. She picked it up, and Thomsen was at the other end.

"We just got the kickback on those prints, and the Feds haven't got them."

Delia repressed an unladylike word. "So that's that. That was all the evidence we had."

"The way the ball bounces sometimes," said Thomsen. "But that kill—it would have been nice to catch up to one like that. Very much the lunatic thing."

"Yes, very much. Well, thanks." So that was that, and there were just no leads to follow on whoever had battered Amanda Phelps—and her dog and cat—to death. They might as well put that into Pending and forget about it. She sat back in the desk chair and massaged her neck muscles; she was stiff from hunching over the typewriter. The end of another unprofitable day, and nearly time to go home. Talk to Nadine's girl friends sometime tomorrow, catch them at school? The order to look at Lila Finch's bank account ought to be coming through tomorrow, and also they could probably contact the city engineers' office. And none of them was thinking that that bank account was all that important now; whatever it had looked like at first, it didn't look now like the elaborate abduction for ransom; but they had to be thorough and look everywhere there was to look.

She was still sitting there staring out the tall windows across the office when Varallo and Forbes came out with the suspect, an unkempt lout, and Forbes took him out and Varallo sat down at his desk and reached for the phone.

"Did you do any good?" asked Delia.

"Bingo," said Varallo. "This one was a good make. He had the gun on him, and he's not very bright. We confused him a little with too many questions at once, and he finally admitted, yeah, that was him at the drugstore, not that he wanted all them pills himself, he don't mess around with that stuff, but you can sell them to other guys. He's out of a job and he wanted to get a nice Christmas present for his girl friend. I think I've just got time to apply for the warrant."

When they looked into O'Connor's office before leaving, the cat was still asleep. Varallo opened another can of cat food and said, "I'd better borrow a couple of bowls from Laura—she ought to have water too." He had left a note for the night watch about their new tenant.

The night watch was amused about the cat, and Rhys was a little worried. His mother bred Cairn terriers, and he'd helped her through a few difficult whelpings; things could go wrong. Cats were usually all right, especially ordinary cats like this one, but you never knew. Of course, if anything did go wrong, Dr. Jepson would come out at the drop of a hat; it was his opinion that animals were more important than people. Rhys liked a nice cat, but unfortunately they already had one, who ruled over the Cairn terriers with a rod of iron and wouldn't be disposed to put up with any upstart kitten.

They didn't get a call until nine-fifty, an address on Glenoaks; when Rhys and Harvey got there, there was a paramedic truck in front of the apartment house. Inside the open front door of the downstairs apartment, the paramedics were just strapping a man onto a gurney. He looked bad; he wasn't a young man, maybe sixty, though it was hard to tell, when he was covered with blood and dirt, and the clothes he had on—a brown suit, white shirt—were torn and muddy. A woman was crying over the gurney.

"Where are you taking him? I want to go with him—I've got to know—"

"Sorry, ma'am—he'll be at the emergency wing, Memorial Hospital."

"I told you his name—Jim Holland—could I see the doctor right away? I'll have to call a cab—"

"You'll have to ask, ma'am. We'd better make it snappy, Sam —he doesn't look good." They carried out the gurney in a hurry, and Rhys started to ask a few elementary questions. She was a sandy-haired woman looking about the same age as the man, wearing a blue chenille bathrobe and bedroom slippers.

"I've got to get dressed, I've got to go there and see how he is —oh, I told him, that stubborn, stubborn man, but he would go out—I told him the post office doesn't empty those boxes at night, it doesn't matter what it says on the lid, but he was bound and determined to mail the letter tonight—stubborn! And getting beat up by one of these muggers—I don't know how he managed to get home—I tried to keep my head—"

"Is he your husband, Mrs. Holland?"

"My brother—it's Miss—there wasn't anything important about the letter, it was just to Bill—our brother up north—but he would go out! And he hadn't any money on him at all, but they took his wristwatch—I've got to call a cab—"

In common humanity they drove her down to the Memorial Hospital. Rhys said on the way back, "The gang members roving around."

"Probably," agreed Harvey. And there was nothing to be done about that: the muggers, gang members or whoever, vanished into the woodwork.

At eleven-thirty they were called out to a burglary: the couple had just come home from the movies and found the place ransacked. It was a cheap apartment on Doran, and they were just young people, the wife obviously pregnant. There hadn't, by the look of the place, been much there to take, but they took down the list: a couple of small appliances, a camera, and—adding insult to injury—a lot of Christmas presents wrapped for mailing. Presents for the family back east. "And they were all on the credit card," she said mournfully.

"I kept telling the manager these damn locks are no good," he said wrathfully. They weren't; the burglar had easily pried open the door with a chisel or something.

When they got back to the office, Hunter said, "The hospital called five minutes ago. The Holland fellow just died."

"Oh, hell," said Rhys. "That's a damn shame. Just out to mail a letter, and one of these tough little punks—and all they got was his wristwatch."

"And," said Harvey, "not one damn thing we can do about it, Bob."

"File the report," said Rhys. Sometimes this was a very discouraging job.

"Well, there you are," said the man from the city engineers' office. His name was Costello. He happened to be the first one Varallo had talked to, and he'd been so intrigued that he had chased right over here with a lot of unwieldy blueprints, which were spread all over Varallo's desk and which nobody but Costello could decipher. "You can see it for yourselves. You think this woman was thrown into the Wash from somewhere here in town? From one of the bridges, you said. Well, my God, it's been carrying a hell of a lot of water." He flattened out one large sheet of blueprint. "And at night—well, she could have been carried right out into the valley by morning, and sure, before anybody might have had a chance to spot her while she was still on the surface, she'd have gone right smack down the underground conduit. You can see it for yourselves." They couldn't make head or tail of the blueprint, where he pointed insistently. "It takes a lot of twists and turns, but it's designed to handle a lot of water fast. They tell me we used to get some damn bad flooding, forty-odd years ago before it was built. But the underground conduit—it's twenty feet high all the way, I doubt if there'd be a chance a body'd get hung up anywhere—and, God, no way to look. If it's somewhere in there, nobody's going to know it until a team of archaeologists starts digging up the ruins of L.A. County five hundred years from now. Otherwise, she'd have been carried right down to the coast, that's where it empties, you know. My God, what a thing to do to anybody! Before the Wash got built, that used to happen now and then, but just by accident. There was a case I heard about from one of the oldtimers in the office—back in the late thirties, in one of the wet years, a fellow was swept right down one of the storm drains at an intersection, and they never did find his body."

O'Connor peered at the blueprints. "Would it be carried out very far, do you know?"

Costello said dubiously, "I couldn't say, might have been. It goes down at quite a speed, you know, and at low tide—hell, I don't know a damn thing about tides—but it could have got taken out quite a way off the coast."

Varallo thanked him. He was disposed to linger and talk about it, but reluctantly he folded up his blueprints and went out. O'Connor said, "Well, we'd better ask the Harbor Patrol."

"That order came in to look at the bank account," said Delia. "It's the Security Pacific branch on North Brand." But they just sat thinking about Lila Finch, possibly tumbling around out in the stormy Pacific, reduced to an unidentifiable corpse. O'Connor was on the phone.

He got handed around to various offices, but finally talked to a Captain Whitney, who could give them something definite. In the last three weeks the Harbor Patrol hadn't come across any floating bodies, he said, and why was Glendale asking? O'Connor told him, and he was even more intrigued than Costello. He was also more knowledgeable about tides and bodies. He said, "If that happened, the body might have got down as far as the coast by daylight, say, and low tide's been anywhere from around five to seven the last few weeks. The chances are, anything coming down that conduit would be drawn a couple of miles out by the time the tide turned. After that you could forget about a body ever turning up. I suppose you've heard about fish—it'd probably be reduced to a skeleton inside twenty-four hours, and broken up in another few days."

"Christ," said O'Connor. He passed that on to Delia and Varallo.

Varallo said, "Well, we'll do a little more spadework on it. There may not be any way to prove she's dead, but if she hasn't written any checks in the last three weeks, and hasn't been seen anywhere, it's a strong presumption. We'll take a look at her bank account."

He and Delia went up to that bank and presented the judicial order to the bank manager, who left them in his office and bustled away to look up records. Delia said, "The Phelps thing is dead, we'll never get anything more on it. And when you think about this new thing, Vic—it seems a very queer place for a murder, the public library, but you know, it wasn't so queer that nobody noticed anything. Goulding says she was stabbed. That's a big place, and the chair where she was sitting was a good way off from any other. And in a library, nobody there would be taking much notice of anything—extraneous. People in the stacks looking for books—at the checkout desk—the librarians busy checking books in and out. A few people sitting around reading. It might have been terribly easy—just lean over her as if he, whoever, was talking to her, shove the knife in, and walk away. If he knew just where to shove it in—or was lucky—she could have died nearly at once, never had a chance to move or make a sound."

"Yes, you can see that."

"And this boy—the all-round athlete—never mind what the parents think, one like that might have been more than annoyed with her for turning him down. He wouldn't be used to girls turning him down, the big hero on campus. And it could very well have been common knowledge that she always went to the library on Saturday. I want to have a look at him."

"Yes, I think so."

The manager came back and laid records in front of them. Half an hour later Varallo straightened up and said, "Well, it just adds to the presumption." There hadn't been any movement in Lila Finch's bank account since the day before Thanksgiving. On that day she'd written a check for twenty-three sixty-five. No record of the payee, of course; all the November checks had been returned to her by mail. Since then nothing: no checks written. Looking back, they had found records in past months of regular payments at the first or last of the month: two sums reoccurred—sixty, and a hundred and thirty dollars. "The gardener and the cleaning woman," said Delia. Other checks at roughly the same dates would be for utility bills. There had seldom been less than eighteen or twenty checks each month. She had paid her Visa account in full, which she could do through the bank, the day before Thanksgiving; it had amounted to something over four hundred dollars.

"And it may be an exercise in futility," said Delia, "but I think you'd better put a stop on all checks on the account. If any should turn up." Because there hadn't been a checkbook in that handbag, and it was conceivable that the unknown burglar-killer might try to use that.

"Yes, of course," said the manager. "This is a terrible thing—Mrs. Finch is one of our oldest accounts—such a very nice woman—yes, of course, we'd better do that."

"Those canceled checks will be at the house," said Delia. "Not that I think they're important. And we haven't seen the gardener yet."

Varallo said, "I'll do that. You want to catch these girl friends of Nadine's. Just as well to talk to them without parents around. Girls that age—"

Delia said soberly, "That's what I thought."

O'Connor was sitting at Varallo's desk at three o'clock, complaining to Jeff Forbes about all that paraphernalia cluttering up his office—"A litter tray yet"—when the desk relayed a call. He picked up the phone and said, "Lieutenant O'Connor."

A rough voice at the other end said, "This is Les Bernhardt, the Acme Garage. The cop on the beat asked us to report any Lincoln Continental with front-end damage. I got one in about an hour ago."

"Goddamn, do we get a break on that? Where are you?"

"Mission Street, South Pasadena. I never saw the guy before, but he left it off and said—"

"Hold everything," said O'Connor. "We'll be over to talk to you."

CHAPTER 6

Bernhardt was as broad and bulky as O'Connor, with a rough-hewn face and a gruff voice. He owned the garage, a big one and a busy one by the number of cars in. He said to O'Connor and Forbes, "I never saw the guy before, we got a lot of regular customers but he's not one of them. He gave the name of William Johnson, but that's not how the Lincoln's registered. Like I say, I remembered what the cop on the beat said, and I looked —naturally I'd have no reason to do that in the ordinary way, but I looked—the registration's in the glove compartment and it says Brian Washburn, a La Cañada address."

"What's the car look like?" asked O'Connor. "He drove in?"

"Yeah, it's running, he left it off and called a cab. I don't give out loaners, too much trouble. He said his wife ran into the driveway gate, well, I wouldn't know." He shrugged. "The left front wheel's way out of alignment and there's a little damage to the underbody. Is it a hit-run?"

"That's just what. Let's have a look," said Forbes.

The Lincoln was parked around at the side of the garage. It was about three years old, and looked clean and well cared for. The damage wasn't visible, and there wasn't any visible blood on the front grill. Forbes said, "Last Wednesday. And all the rain. But the lab can do miracles."

"I think," said O'Connor, "just to be on the safe side, we'll have it towed in and let the lab boys have a look." He called the station. "And thanks very much, Bernhardt."

"No trouble," said Bernhardt. "Have to cooperate with you guys."

La Cañada was a very expensive, high-class residential area, and the house was a two-story Spanish place with an upper balcony, a glimpse of a covered swimming pool off to one side, and a manicured front lawn. On the wide front porch O'Connor pushed the bell and they waited. Unhurriedly the door opened and they faced an attractive blond woman in the forties, smartly dressed in a beige pantsuit.

"We're looking for Mr. Washburn," said O'Connor genially. "Is he here?"

She said, "Well, no, of course he's at the office. What's it about?"

"Just a little business," said Forbes. They didn't show the badges; they didn't want her calling to warn him. "Where is his office?"

She was looking puzzled. She said sharply, "Why, Pacific Savings and Loan in Glendale, if it's business I should think you'd know—"

O'Connor gave her his sharklike grin. "Thanks very much, ma'am."

It was one of the new high-rise buildings on North Brand. Pacific Savings and Loan occupied the entire ground floor. They went in and asked the security guard about Washburn, and he said with a little surprise, "Mr. Washburn's one of the directors, you'll find his office back there," and pointed. Past the row of tellers' cages along one side was a row of labeled doors. O'Connor opened the one embellished in gold letters *B. J. Washburn,* and they found themselves in an expensively furnished reception office with a desk, a sharply modern low couch and chairs. The expensive furnishings included a platinum blonde at the desk. She had a long and inquisitive nose, blood-red fingernails, and a haughty nasal voice. She told them they'd have to make an appointment.

"I don't think so," said O'Connor, and brought out the badge. Her eyes sharpened but she didn't say anything, just got up and went through the door at the rear of the anteroom. After a minute she came back and nodded curtly at them, leaving that door open. They went into a large square room even more lavishly appointed. The big Danish modern desk was at right angles to the window, with a view over a little neat strip of landscaping at the side of the building—bushes and lawn.

Washburn was sitting at the desk; he didn't get up to greet them. He was a big beefy man about fifty, with thinning brown hair and sharp aquiline features. He was very sharply dressed in a conventional dark gray business suit, a white shirt, and dark tie.

"Mr. Washburn," said O'Connor formally, "you left a Lincoln Continental at the Acme Garage in South Pasadena this morning, for repairs to the front end. It was a little out of the way for you, but that's understandable." Washburn didn't move or speak. "It was pretty damned foolish to give a false name, but of course, you don't know one damn thing about how police operate, do you? That's the car that ran a red light on Brand Boulevard last Wednesday afternoon and killed a young woman named Jean Hoffman. It's being towed in to the police garage right now, and there just could be a little blood on it somewhere, our lab men will be taking a look. Is there anything you'd like to say, Mr. Washburn?"

He did move then, swiveling around in the desk chair away from them, and he said, "Oh, my God. I didn't think you could find out—it was a chance to take—I'm sorry. I'm sorry. I've been through hell over this. So you know it was the car. I was afraid—"

O'Connor said coldly, "Would you like to tell us about it?"

"I don't know what there is to tell—nothing like this ever happened to me before. I never meant to do a thing like that, my God, I couldn't believe it had happened." He bent his head in his hands. "I couldn't tell my wife—there was a story in the paper about her, it said husband and two children—I've been through hell. It just happened—I've always been a good driver, never had a moving violation ticket—"

"So how did it happen, Mr. Washburn?" asked Forbes gently.

He said in a dull voice, "I'd been to lunch—it was business—a couple of men from our Hollywood branch office—we're opening a new office out in the Valley, it was about that. We were at the Tam o' Shanter Inn." That was over in Atwater. "I'd only had a couple of drinks, well, maybe three, I don't remember. I can hold my liquor all right, I wasn't tight, I couldn't have been. I admit I was driving too fast, I had an appointment, I was in a hurry to get back to the office—"

"And you'll be familiar with the traffic lights on Brand, but you just weren't noticing that one?"

"God, I don't know. I just don't know. It just happened. I—no, I was in the left lane, I just didn't see the light, and before I knew it I was on top of the woman. She was just a blur, it was a dark day—raining—and I guess I just panicked, I gave it the gun and got away—by the time I got to the office parking lot I was wishing to hell I'd stopped, but it was too late—there's a kind of instinct for self-preservation—" He sat up.

"So there is," said O'Connor. "And we've got in some damn stiff new rules, penalties for drunk driving. Just maybe you were thinking about that, Mr. Washburn. We'll be hearing the names of the men you were with and just maybe they'll tell us you had four or five drinks, and not much lunch. Will they?" Washburn just looked a little more haggard.

After a long, dragging minute he said, "What happens now?"

"You're going to jail," said O'Connor. "You'll get bail, and your wife can come and get you out, probably tomorrow. There'll be a hearing in court, and you'll lose your license and come in for a heavy fine, but that's the least of it. There'll be a charge of manslaughter, the degree will be up to the judge, and I'd like to think you'll do a little time for it. We'll take you in now."

Washburn got up without a word, got his hat and coat out of a small closet, and Forbes took his arm. They led him out past the hard-faced secretary, who stared and said, "You've got an appointment with Mr. Fancher at four-thirty, sir."

He said quietly, "You'll have to tell him I can't make it, Marion."

They delivered him to the jail, told him he could call his wife.

O'Connor said, "And the hell of a lot of good it does to Jean Hoffman, Jeff, but at least we caught up to him. If there was any sense to the judicial system, he'd be legally responsible to pay compensation to the husband and kids."

Forbes agreed. "Let's hope it's taught him some kind of lesson, but I wouldn't bet on it."

Katz and Poor had just got back from looking at a daylight break-in at an apartment on Grandview Avenue when they were sent out again. This one was at a single house on Howard Street, one of the blocks east of town which were rapidly changing their faces. Where once all these blocks had held modest single houses, some with little rental units in the rear, those were fast coming down to make room for large new apartment buildings and condominiums. On this block, only about half of the original houses were left; across the street was a six-story apartment, still new and raw looking, no landscaping around it yet, and half a block up, construction was underway on another about the same size. The address they had been given was one of the original old places, a bungalow with a wide front porch, and the householder was waiting for them on the porch. The squad-car man had called in and gone back to the station at the end of his tour. The householder was a tall, horse-faced woman; her name was Sarah Vinson. She was wearing a nurse's white uniform. She said crisply, "Are you the detectives? I just got home at three-thirty and discovered I'd had a burglar. The crime rate is disgraceful! I know the police do their best, but it's really outrageous, Glendale's always been a nice, quiet, safe town, it's all these aliens and the lower-class people coming in from Hollywood and Pasadena—we never used to have many Negroes here, and Mexicans moving in in droves, I don't like to sound prejudiced but one has to look at realities."

Katz said, "Yes, ma'am, we'll take a look. You can give us a list of what's missing. Had you been out of the house for long?"

"Certainly, since six-thirty this morning as usual. I'm an LVN at the Sunset Convalescent Home on Colorado, I'm on the seven-to-three shift. I haven't had a good look yet, but I can tell you right off that my microwave oven's gone, and my camera, and my tape recorder. The lock on the front door's all right, he got in the back bedroom window, the screen's been pried off."

They looked, and it was the usual mess. In both bedrooms, drawers had been dumped hastily, the contents pawed through. The kitchen hadn't been touched, or the living room. The window in the back bedroom hadn't been locked—Miss Vinson looked a little crestfallen about that, admitted she ought to have had the lock fixed. "But I won't be here much longer and it didn't seem worthwhile—this whole block's being cleared, you know, the houses are due to come down by next March—an upset, I've lived here forty years, it was my parents' house, but these things happen. I haven't signed the papers yet but I'm supposed to next week."

Katz looked out the kitchen window. There was a little frame house in the rear. "Does anybody live there, Miss Vinson?"

"Certainly," she said crisply. "I rent it to a very nice young man, Tim Canfield, he's one of the night orderlies at the Community Hospital. Naturally he has to sleep during the day, I don't suppose he heard a thing."

Poor had wandered back into the back bedroom. "Hey, Joe," he said, "come here."

"You spot something?" Katz went to join him. Poor was leaning out the open window.

"Look at that," and he pointed. Below the window, caught on the thorns of a struggling rosebush, was a little tangle of yellow knitting yarn. Miss Vinson peered out.

"Why, that's the yarn I got the other day, I'd just been winding it, getting ready to make a cardigan for my sister's birthday in February, yellow's her favorite color—however did it get there? And just a little bit of it—"

Poor's nose twitched. "Where was it, Miss Vinson?"

"Why, on the table by the window—"

Katz said, "For God's sake." He made for the front door, Poor and Miss Vinson after him. He went around the side of the house to that window. The little tangle of yarn wasn't very big, and a trail of yarn, a single strand, led from it toward the rear of the house. "What in the name of goodness—" said Miss Vinson.

Katz didn't know anything about knitting, but evidently the yarn had been loosely wound and had unraveled neatly as it was pulled along. It led them down the side of the house, around into the backyard, and up to the door of the little house in the rear. It disappeared under the rather loose-fitting front door. "Oh, my goodness," said Miss Vinson.

Katz tried the door and it was unlocked. They all went into a minute living room. The yarn continued across the room past an open door, and they followed it in. In an even tinier bedroom, holding only a single bed, a dresser, and a straight chair, the yarn led directly to a pair of brown pants laid across the chair. A man was sound asleep in the bed. Katz picked up the pants. The belt had been left threaded through the loops, and the end of the strand of yarn was firmly wedged in the sharp edge of a fancy silver belt buckle. Katz and Poor burst out laughing.

"It caught on his belt when he went back through the window," said Poor, "and he never noticed it. I'll be damned."

"But, Tim Canfield—he's such a nice young man—"

The man in the bed rolled over and said, "Huh—who's there?" and sat up. He was a boyish-looking, rather handsome young fellow with a narrow chin and a snub nose. He stared at them.

Katz said, "You'd better get dressed. You're going to jail."

He woke up further. "What the hell?"

"You left a little trail behind you when you burglarized the front house," said Poor. Katz held up the pants, the yellow yarn dangling from the belt. Canfield stared at it, at the yarn leading across the floor.

"Breaking into my house—stealing my things—I thought you were such a good tenant!" said Miss Vinson indignantly.

Canfield said frankly, "I'll be damned. I will be damned. I never noticed that damned stuff."

They didn't have to look far for the loot; it was all neatly stacked up in a corner of the living room. Katz was still chortling when they got back to the office.

"Honestly, Miss Riordan, there isn't anything to tell you," Sue Norman had said to Delia. "It's just like we've been telling you, Nadine never was in any trouble of any kind, everybody liked Nadine."

Cindy White, with just a small trace of resentment in her voice, said, "We sort of thought she needed a shrink, act the way she had to Mark Schafer, I mean, imagine collecting one like Mark, me, I'd of flipped, but she was playing it real cool—"

Delia had talked to the girls' vice principal at Hoover High, and she had let Delia use her office. She was a shrewd-eyed, sensible-looking woman, very shocked about Nadine, and she didn't even ask to sit in on the questioning, which was tactful.

Betty Cannon said, "Well, I sort of saw her point, Cindy. Jim and I double-dated with them a couple of times, and I might not be as big a brain as Nadine, but Mark really is sort of dumb. You know he'd have flunked math if some of the rest of the team hadn't helped him—they really need him on the team."

Delia looked at the girls consideringly. Like Nadine, these girls were probably the cream of the crop as high school kids went these days. In the general term, nice girls. Not participants in the promiscuous sex, the drugs. Contrary to statistics, there were still a lot like that. They had been shocked about Nadine; they hadn't heard about it until she told them, and Nadine had been a close friend to all of them, but at this age excitement over an unusual and unexpected death was mingled with shock. They had shed a few conventional tears, told Delia what a super girl Nadine had been, really a sweet girl, and it was just awful her getting killed like that. But they couldn't tell her any reason anybody might have wanted to hurt Nadine—she'd never had trouble with anybody at school, she'd never had any fights with anybody over anything. They had asked eager questions, accepted that she wouldn't tell them any details. They looked at her with limpid, honest eyes, and she thought they were being honest. Three of them were dark, the Cannon girl a rather striking blonde, all of them at least as pretty as Nadine.

"What about Mark Schafer?" she asked. "I understand Nadine had turned him down lately when he asked her for dates."

Sue Norman said, "That's right, and frankly we all thought she was crazy, I mean, you don't expect a guy to be a genius if he's got other things going for him, do you? It wasn't like he was expecting her to marry him and spend the rest of her life with him. You've got to have some social life."

Linda Barlow said, "That's right, but that was Nadine for you, she didn't really care. Sure, we were good friends, but I really think she'd rather sit at home and read a book than go out on a date. With anybody. She was a brain, you know."

Delia talked to them a little longer and let them go; she didn't think they had anything important to tell, no secrets to reveal about that quiet, ambitious girl Nadine Parker. She found the vice principal in the outer office and talked to her a little more. She said there really wasn't much to tell about Nadine, except that she'd been the kind of student every teacher hoped to have, the kind of girl all too uncommon these days in public school—never any discipline problems, an excellent attendance record, on the staff of the school newspaper and the yearbook, member of the Literature Club. Not the kind of girl who was wildly popular, had a great many friends, that wasn't her type. She said regretfully, "I think she'd have made her mark in the world, possibly as a talented writer or musician. It's a terrible thing when a bright, intelligent person like that is taken so young. And it's just beyond my imagination why or how she could have been killed like that. Do the police have any idea at all?"

"Not at the moment, Mrs. Franklin."

The three-o'clock bell rang, marking the end of the school day. She found her way to the office of the boys' vice principal, whose name was Aarons, and talked to him about Mark Schafer. He was an ascetic-looking man with wintry gray eyes, and he said dryly, "Sometimes our values get a little confused, Miss Riordan. I don't know the boy well, but of course I've heard something from his teachers—from—ah—our athletic coach, Mr. Bogard. We try to demand some minimum standards of scholarship, if that word means anything anymore, but really who is to say what it's worth? With so much emphasis on financial success, all the fawning adulation of the illiterate rock stars and the like, who are we to feel superior to a boy like that, call him stupid? He'll probably go on to become a professional athlete in some big league and make so much money that it won't matter whether he can spell a two-syllable word or remember any historical dates."

"Have there ever been any discipline problems with him, any trouble with other students?"

"Oh, no, he's quite a good boy, what you'd call well brought-up. I believe his father is a physician." And Delia thought instantly, the Schafer boy might not be very bright academically, but in a doctor's house there might be illustrated medical books, and he could have found out just where to shove that knife in. Or was that woolgathering?

Aarons said, "I take it you'd like to talk to him. I really don't think he's the type to commit a murder—though teenagers can be an unknown quantity—and that's a dreadful thing, a girl like that killed—he'll probably be at football practice now, I'll put a call in to the gym."

She talked to Mark Schafer in the coach's office there and wasn't sure how she felt about him. On the surface he was just a big, good-natured kid, conventionally handsome, with curly blond hair, regular features. He said awkwardly that he'd heard about Nadine just a while ago, Betty Cannon had told him after his last class, and he felt just awful about it. "She was an awful nice girl, I can't believe it, that somebody'd want to kill her. I really liked Nadine."

"You'd dated her a few times, hadn't you?"

"Yeah, some."

"But lately she'd been turning you down."

"Oh," he said. "You heard about that. Yeah, that's right, I guess she thought, well, like I wasn't good enough for her. I mean smart enough. She was a nice girl, see, she wouldn't say it like that, but I guess that's the way she felt. But geez, well, way I look at it, there are different ways of being smart, see?"

"So you weren't mad at her for turning you down?"

He looked a little mildly surprised. "Geez, I guess not exactly mad—I was sorry about it—I liked Nadine real good. Say, the police don't think I had anything to do with it? Killing *Nadine*— Geez, that'd be just crazy, I wouldn't kill anybody."

"Did you know that she usually went to the library on Saturday afternoon?"

He nodded. "She liked to read. I don't see what anybody gets out of it, but like I say, there are different ways of being smart. I got other things going for me." He was regarding her rather watchfully now.

"Where were you on Saturday afternoon?" asked Delia easily.

He stared at her and licked his lips. "Say, you don't really think I'd of done anything to Nadine? Betty said she'd got the idea she was knifed or something—that's real weird, it doesn't seem like nothing real—it's just crazy, think I'd maybe do a thing like that! Well, Saturday—it was raining, I didn't go anyplace, I just stayed home and watched TV."

"Was anybody else there?"

"My dad was at a medical seminar in San Diego. My mom and my sister Della went out shopping, I guess they came home about four."

"Do you have a car?"

"Yeah, I got an old heap—say, you don't really think—" He was definitely and transparently alarmed now, but looked more angry than frightened.

"We have to talk to everybody who knew her, Mark. It doesn't necessarily mean we're suspecting you."

"Oh. I guess so. I just can't believe it, Nadine getting killed. She was an awful nice girl. I liked Nadine a lot."

But, by that, he could have been at the library, and nobody the wiser. Nadine had called her mother about one-thirty and had been found dead roughly an hour later, or less. He'd been home alone. He could have been brooding over her rejection of him—as Aarons said, teenagers could be unknown quantities, coping with adult motives for the first time and yet not quite balanced adults.

And if he had done it, would there ever be a way to prove it? Delia sat in the car for a few minutes, ruminating about these things all up in the air. The Phelps thing—that was past praying for, just the anonymous lunatic kill. One like that very conceivably might kill again, and if he did, next time they might get a lead; and they might not too. And if their hunch was right about Lila Finch, and her body had wound up food for fishes out at sea, there'd likely never be any handle on that, as to who had— probably quite inadvertently—killed her. The Myricks would have to wait seven years to get legal presumption of the death and claim her property; she had probably left a will in favor of her niece. As far as all the heists went, some they won and some they lost; it was just how the cards fell. The elderly man mugged —what was his name, Holland—there was just no point in trying to work that at all; there was never any catching up to the muggers. It might very well have been a few gang members jumping him on impulse, or somebody else doped up or wanting money for a fix. Nobody would ever know.

She started the car and drove back downtown. It was still gray and cold. In the lobby of the station, as she came past the newspaper racks her eye caught part of a headline, and she stopped and turned back. The talk got around, intentionally or not, and eventually the press had heard something. The daily edition of the Glendale *News-Press* was just out, and on the right of the front page was a prominent headline: GLENDALE

WOMAN VANISHES. Delia rummaged for change, deposited a quarter in the slot, and abstracted a paper. The press had obviously been talking to the Myricks, but that wouldn't do any harm; the publicity just might turn up a few fresh facts.

And it was strange that when they'd been thinking about Lila Finch, speculating on what might have happened to her, and knowing quite a lot about her—and how queer she'd have thought it, a lot of strangers knowing her daily routine, talking to her friends, questioning her servants—that not until now had they seen a picture of her. Carla Myrick would have given the picture to the press, and it was reproduced under the headline. Delia stood there looking at it, and for a fraction of a second, a small pang struck her heart and she thought of that body out in the Pacific. Which was silly, because it didn't matter what happened to a body, the essential person had just gone somewhere else—and this woman had lived a full and happy life, where Nadine Parker had been killed before she'd had a chance to live much of a life at all. But she stood there for another minute, looking at the reproduced photograph.

It said, "recent photograph"; well, it might be or not. But Lila Finch didn't look sixty-eight. It was a head-and-shoulders photograph, a three-quarter profile. She had been a very good-looking woman, with light hair in a smart modern coiffure, a pretty, roundish face with a tip-tilted nose, a wide, pleasant mouth, and large, expressive eyes. For no reason Delia shivered suddenly; something walking over her grave.

She took the paper upstairs. Varallo, Forbes, and O'Connor were just sitting around talking; they looked at the picture with interest.

"I finally chased down that gardener, Galetti," said Varallo. "He looks like a perfectly honest man. He hadn't seen her in at least a month, but he says there wasn't anything unusual about that. He comes every Wednesday, mows the lawn, trims hedges and so on, whatever needs doing, and goes away. He sends her a monthly bill and she sends him a check."

"All very natural," said Delia. She told them the handful of nothing she'd gleaned at Hoover High School. "I don't know about the Schafer boy. On the surface he's a little too stupid to be true."

Varallo said without enthusiasm, "Talk to the people at the library again—chase down the regulars in around the right time, that the librarians remember."

"Nobody was noticing anything, Vic. There's nothing more to get. The Schafer kid could have done it, or he couldn't. A random lunatic could have done it. We'll probably never know." Delia lit a cigarette moodily.

"The latest forecast says more rain tomorrow," said Forbes.

"Thank you, Pollyanna," said Delia. "And thank God for automatic dryers." Tomorrow was her day off; well, at least it would be a change, doing all the necessary domestic chores, the laundry, the shopping, the appointment at the hairdresser's.

"I don't know what the hell to get Katy for Christmas," said O'Connor gloomily. "She doesn't go much for jewelry. Vince'll be satisfied with a couple of new toy cars—I think he's an incipient mechanic—and he refuses to believe in Santa Claus anyway. But Katy—" Nobody offered any helpful suggestions. "She's been talking about a new electric stove, but it seems damned prosaic for a Christmas present." He passed a hand over his bulldog jaw, as usual in need of a shave. "Well, maybe something'll come to me."

"Girls are easier than boys," said Jeff Forbes sleepily. Their little girl had just turned two, Delia remembered. Now that she came to think, she'd never met Forbes's wife Joan. It was another queer thing—all of them working together on the daily routine, on an intimate basis, yet gaps between.

Varallo stood up and yawned. "I'm going home early. Gil called in a while ago, he's been on a wild goose chase to hell and gone down to Santa Monica and couldn't find the suspect. He's heading in, and it's getting on for end of shift." There was a general move to leave.

"At least something accomplished, something done," said O'Connor. "We caught up to Mr. Washburn."

"And Joe caught up with a burglar," said Varallo. "Oh, my God, Delia, you didn't hear about that—the funniest damn thing—" Delia heard about it and laughed dutifully. She was still thinking about Nadine Parker, the random waste of that, and Lila Finch.

But one of the rules was that you couldn't take the job home with you, get emotionally involved. They all trooped downstairs together and into the parking lot. It was already fully dark, the big arc lights on in the lot, and it wasn't quite so cold. Forbes sniffed the air. "More rain on the way all right."

It was Hunter's night off. When Rhys and Harvey came in, Rhys went into O'Connor's office to look at the cat. The cat, accepting human attention as her just due, had settled down smugly in her carton and, with all creature comforts to hand, had no intention of venturing back to the outside world. Varallo or somebody had opened another can of cat food and cleaned up the litter tray, and there was fresh milk in a china bowl. The cat opened one green eye and purred for Rhys.

They didn't have to wait long for a first call, and it was another repeat: a heist at a jewelry store out on Broadway. The proprietor had been alone, just about to close, when they'd come in and showed a gun, cleaned out all three showcases. "I hadn't started to put stuff away in the safe yet—there were two of them, pretty young guys, Latin types, one of them had a little mustache—" That pair again. He said doubtfully he might recognize a picture. Nobody had yet, but he might, if either of them was in Records. He agreed to make up a list of what they'd got and come in in the morning to make a statement and look at mug shots.

They went back to the office and waited around some more. And the radio made a background. There was another pile-up on the freeway, probably a bad one with two ambulances called.

At ten-thirty, Communications relayed word of another heist. The address was San Fernando Road. Of course, there were heists all over the place these days, but Rhys couldn't place any retail store in that block, and when they got there it turned out to be the bus depot for the local transit company. The squad car was at the curb outside the high chain link fence, and the uniformed man was waiting for them at the open gate. It was Steiner, and as they came up, he started to laugh.

"This is a damn funny place for a heist," said Harvey.

"Oh, it didn't happen here," said Steiner, giggling. "Wait till you hear about it—" The big yard was full of the clumsy yellow city buses parked in orderly rows. It was all dark and quiet, but at one side of the yard was a square little wooden building with a light showing. Steiner led them over there. "There's nobody here at night but a security guard, this is the dispatcher's office and they use it for the lost and found department, things people leave on buses, you know. Oh, wait till you hear about this one!" He was still laughing.

Inside the little office were two men. One of them was the uniformed security guard, a big, heavy-shouldered fellow about fifty, and they could see he'd made a comfortable if homely place for himself here for his lonely nights. There was a single cot, and a padded rocking chair drawn up close to a forced-air wall heater. There was a paperback Western open and face down on the rocking chair, and on the table beside it a package of cigarettes, an ashtray, a package of salted peanuts, and a couple of candy bars.

The other man was standing beside the chair, as close to the heater as he could get, and as the other three men came in, the guard was saying sharply, "Don't you dare sit down in my chair, Mike—it's the only place I got to sit—oh, my God, you're dripping it all over the floor—"

Rhys and Harvey stared at the second man. He was stark naked, and he was covered all over with what looked like green slime. He was a fattish man somewhere around the guard's age, with a bald head, and his tanned face contrasted strangely with the pale white of the rest of his skin, where you could see any skin, and he was shivering violently.

"I can't help it, Joe—my God, how'm I going to get home?"

"What the hell is all this?" asked Rhys, and the man looked up at them. He had a plain, bulldog face.

Steiner said, "This is Mike Andrews. He's had quite an experience."

"Experience!" said Andrews in an outraged voice. "Are these more cops? Well, I guess there's no way you could do anything about it. Experience! I tell you, I been driving a bus for the city for twenty years, and I never had worse than a lady starting labor pains once—my God, just look at the mess I'm in, my wife'll have seven fits, but I better call her and get her to bring me some clothes—"

"What happened to you, Mr. Andrews?" asked Harvey.

He sneezed. "I'll bet I got a cold. I already told the other cop. Well, I'd made my last run—we shut down pretty early, you know, even at this time of year we don't get all that many people riding the buses—and I'm on my way to bring the bus back here and leave it. I guess it'd be about nine-forty. I catch the light at Central and Maple, there's nothing much around there that time of night, hardly any people in the street, and I stopped for the light, and there are these two guys, they came up and rapped on the door, I should open it—so naturally I step on the pedal and open it, and I sing out that I'm out of service, not taking any passengers, but they pile right in—one of them was carrying a big paper bag like a market bag—and they hit me on the head with something, I don't know what, but it put me right out—I've got a hell of a lump on my head—" He felt it tenderly. "And I don't know how long I was out, but when I started to come to, the two guys were just getting out of the bus, and one of them yells at me, he says, 'So long, you poor fish'— and I'm in this goddamned mess! They'd smashed open the money box, there might've been a hundred bucks or so in it, in half dollars and quarters—you got to have the exact change, you know—and they'd stripped me naked, took my uniform and underwear and poured this damned stuff all over me—I guess that was what was in the bag—"

"What the hell is it?" asked Rhys.

Steiner was laughing again. "It's tartar sauce—must be forty bottles of tartar sauce—"

"My God," said Harvey, and started to laugh too.

"And what the hell can I do but drive in? The bus is a mess— all over the seat—and when I got here Joe wouldn't let me in at first—"

"I thought it was one of those green men from Mars," said the guard. Everybody but Andrews started to laugh.

"Yeah, I suppose I look damn funny, but I got to get home—" In the end, the guard called his wife, and she brought him some clothes and a couple of towels to clean up the tartar sauce until he could take a bath. He couldn't give them any description of the two men, hadn't got a good look.

"We seem to be getting some queer ones lately," said Rhys. "Now that is one for the books." And of course nothing to do about it.

Arturo Lopez was still technically a rookie; he'd been on the force just over a year. It was an interesting job, he liked it, and if the night shift got boring, well, somebody had to do it. He'd done a spell on swing shift, which was more interesting, and just gone on nights last month.

He'd been cruising around ever since midnight and hadn't had a single call. But at two-forty, Communications sent him to an address on Milford, unknown trouble. When he got there, to a single house on a quiet block, he found two women on the verge of hysterics. One of them was an old lady in a wheelchair, the other one a wild-eyed woman clutching her bathrobe around her.

"She's walking, it's her ghost! I got up to get Mrs. Doty a pain pill and I saw the lights next door—there was a woman just got murdered there last week, Mrs. Phelps—and they always say people murdered come back and *walk*—"

"Don't be foolish, Ida," said the other woman. "It's a burglar."

Lopez had the fleeting thought that a ghost wouldn't require electric lights, but he went to check. There were certainly lights in the house next door, and the front door was locked, but he went around to the back and found that somebody had broken in—the glass pane in the upper part of that door was smashed, and the door was standing open where somebody had reached in to unlock it.

He went through the kitchen cautiously and into a big combination living-dining room. There was a tall, elderly man there, an ordinary-looking man who looked at him and said, "You are a policeman. We have to believe that the temporal forces of law are on the right side. Perhaps you can help me. She was a witch, you see—she put a curse on my wife and killed her—it says, *Thou shalt not suffer a witch to live*—but after I had destroyed her, it came to me that there would be all her wicked potions and magic recipes here—filth—" He crossed himself reverently. "And I came to destroy them—"

Lopez felt his skin crawl. "Yes, sir," he said. "I'll help you. If you'll just come along with me, we'll—we'll take care of the problem."

CHAPTER 7

"The Traffic man wasn't exactly sure what to do with him," said Forbes to Varallo on Tuesday morning. He'd got here first and found Rhys's report. "The night watch had left. But the guy was obviously off his rocker, and the Traffic man ferried him down to the psychiatric ward at Memorial Hospital and left him. The two women identified him, by the way—it's the next-door neighbor, a man by the name of Adam Lowder."

"For God's sake," said Varallo in astonishment.

"Well," said Forbes dryly, "we said that was a lunatic. It looks like it, in spades. We'd better see if we can talk to him."

They went down to the hospital together. Hospitals kept early hours, but their shifts didn't coincide with those of the police. They talked to a couple of interns, a brisk nurse in a cubicle of an office at the end of a long silent hall. One of the interns said, "We were told it was a police case. Of course, we haven't had a chance to evaluate him yet, I don't know much about it, just came on a couple of hours ago."

The nurse said, "By the chart he's been quiet as a lamb, no trouble. He went to sleep right away without any medication, and he ate a good breakfast an hour ago. He isn't talking much —I suppose it's all right to let you see him."

Adam Lowder was sitting in a straight chair at the side of a narrow hospital bed in a tiny room. He looked ill and gray, but quite nonviolent. Varallo said quietly, "Mr. Lowder, we're police officers, we'd like to talk to you about Mrs. Phelps."

He nodded politely. They had taken away his clothes, and he was wearing a flimsy hospital gown. "Police," he said. "Oh yes, that will be the secular arm of the law. It was a police officer brought me here, he assured me the matter was being investigated, but I would like to see Father Patrick too—it is St. Anthony's Church in Burbank—if you'd be so kind to inform him, he should hear about it. I realize now I should have told him about it before."

"About Mrs. Phelps?" asked Forbes.

"Yes, that's right," said Lowder. He sounded quite sensible, but his eyes were remote and unfocused. He sat forward, his bony hands clasped on his knees. "I have been reading Mr. Montague Summers' book on the subject. You know the Church"—he crossed himself—"has always had a great deal of trouble coping with witchcraft. *Thou shalt not suffer a witch to live.* Yes, I had begun to suspect her when my dear wife was so ill, and of course, she gave herself away. She had pretended to be friendly, my wife had thought of her as a friend. But she gave herself away, and then I knew."

"Knew what, Mr. Lowder?" asked Varallo.

"Why, that she was a witch—a servant of Satan—and she had put a curse on Myra—my wife—and killed her. It must have been that, she faded away so quickly. It came to me in a flash when the woman said that to me, that morning."

"What did she say to you, Mr. Lowder?" asked Varallo.

"You will inform Father Patrick that I must see him? I realize the official authorities must know all about it, of course. I realized the truth at once. I'd suspected her, and that morning when I was out in my backyard and she was there next door—with those two creatures—and she boasted about it!" He shivered. "She talked about them, she said she was so fond of them—*fond*—and they understood every word she said. So of course I knew they were her familiars—servants of Satan who aided her in her black ways. Such filth, such enemies of the Church, had to be destroyed. I destroyed them—I destroyed them all—but I think now I should have gone to Father Patrick first, allowed the Church to arrange the matter. Yes, I should have done that." He went on, nodding to himself. "You'll tell Father Patrick? I should like to see him at once."

Varallo and Forbes went out to the corridor and Varallo said, "God."

"So now we know," said Forbes. "I wonder how long he's been the complete lunatic, nobody suspecting it."

"Maybe just since the wife died, it sent him right off. My God, that poor innocent woman with her cat and dog—"

They talked to the interns and spelled it out for them. There would be an official psychiatric evaluation, and in the end he'd be sent up to Atascadero, the institution for the criminally insane. They'd have to find out if there were any relatives; they didn't know much about the man.

Forbes dropped Varallo at the office to start an initial report on it, and went down to Milford Street. The Lowder house was unlocked, and he went in and looked around. There were a lot of religious statues standing around. He couldn't find an address book; the place was neat and clean enough, a shabbily furnished house, anonymous. Then he remembered the priest, and looked up St. Anthony's Church in Burbank. He drove over there, and when he got there he wondered if the priest would be here on a weekday, how to find him if he wasn't. However, the priest was there, prosaically busy over some paperwork in a little office at the rear of the church. He was a middle-aged man with a lantern jaw and gold-framed spectacles, and he listened to Forbes with dismay.

"Dear me," he said, "what a sad thing." He took off his glasses to polish them with his handkerchief. "Yes, of course I can tell you something about him, he and his wife had been parishioners here for many years—very faithful church members. No, I'm afraid there aren't any relatives at all, they hadn't any children. Mr. Lowder had worked all his life as a printer, he had his own business until he retired a few years ago. What a very sad and dreadful thing, murdering that innocent woman. I had better go and see him, give him what consolation I can. Yes, they owned the house, I've no idea what happens in a case like this, whether the property will be consigned to a conservatorship or what—I dare say it doesn't matter. I suppose I'd be allowed to see him?"

Forbes said, "He'll be transferred to a straight psychiatric facility, probably sometime today, probably the one at Norwalk. I don't know—the head-doctors will be examining him."

"Yes, of course. Dear me. He seemed quite rational on Sunday. How little we do know of our fellow creatures, Mr. Forbes."

Varallo hadn't started to write the report, was telling O'Connor about Lowder, when last night's heist victim, the jewelry store owner, came in to make a statement and give them a list of the loot. His name was Goebel, and he agreed to look at some pictures but said he wasn't sure he'd recognize either of them. Gonzales took him downtown to R. and I. Then a couple of autopsy reports came in, and Varallo glanced over them. James Holland, the mugging victim, had died of head wounds inflicted with some kind of blunt weapon, his skull fractured in several places. The girl, Nadine Parker, had died of a single knife wound. The knife had had a very narrow blade about eight inches long, and it had penetrated the heart. Goulding's opinion was that that could have been just blind chance; few people would have the exact knowledge to locate the heart so accurately. The girl had been a virgin, and otherwise a very healthy specimen. "A hell of a thing," said Varallo to himself. And all up in the air. He kicked it around with O'Connor a little and had just uncovered his typewriter when Burt called him.

"Look, we aren't going to give you anything on this Finch thing. The house had been kept pretty clean, but prints can stay some places for a long time. You gave us some names, and we already had the Myrick couple's prints. We don't know Finch's for sure, but we can take it that the ones we picked up in the bedroom are probably hers. We lifted just one of Mrs. Myrick's in the living room, a lot of unusable partials, and a few of the Espinosa woman's. I went over to get hers and her son's, and they gave me a rough time—objected to being treated like criminals. Her prints were in the kitchen, a couple in the bedroom and living room."

"Which says nothing," said Varallo.

"Nope. Natural they should be. We didn't find any of the son's anyplace. There's no blood in the house, nothing to point you any direction."

"Hell. No, it's all up in the air," said Varallo. "And it looks as if it'll stay that way."

"Sorry," said Burt. "We can't make bricks without straw."

Varallo finally got down to the report on Lowder. It was, of course, raining again. He finished it by lunchtime, just as Forbes came back. Katz and Poor were out, and O'Connor said Wallace and Boswell had gone over to Glendale High chasing a reported seller on the campus; the principal had called in. He went out to lunch with Varallo and Forbes, to the coffee shop down the street. "But you didn't hear about that other thing last night," he said over a sandwich. "I suppose you could call it a heist—the goddamnedest thing I ever heard of—this bus driver, for God's sake." That gave them all a laugh, but of course there wasn't anything to do about it.

Delia got back from the hairdresser's about three o'clock and called Laura just for a little conversation. She'd done the laundry and changed the bed that morning, and stopped on the way home to do the week's marketing. Laura was chatty, but presently Delia was saying firmly, "No, Laura, it's very nice of you but no. I'll come over and have a drink with you on Christmas Eve, but Christmas Day is for the family, you don't want outsiders. It's just lucky it's Vic's day off. We never did much anyway, Alex feeling the way he did about religion. And I'll have to be at the office all day." Like a few other people, cops couldn't count on having Christmas off. Laura tried to argue but Delia wouldn't give in. She had a couple of presents for the children; on the rare occasions when the Varallos wanted to go out, she stayed with the children, and they called her Aunt Delia quite naturally. But Christmas Day was for the family.

Gonzales came back after lunch and said Goebel hadn't picked out any mug shots. They hadn't expected him to. The rain had settled down to a steady drizzle, and when Boswell and Wallace came back, they looked very wet. They'd been talking to a lot of the kids on the high school campus and had odds and ends of information about somebody with pot to sell hanging around off campus several days a week.

"We just looked in to report," said Boswell, "we're going to stake it out, we got a description of his car." O'Connor said restlessly he might as well go along. And even if they picked up the seller, he'd get the tap on the wrist and be back on the street in no time, and there'd be a dozen to take his place.

For the moment, Varallo and Forbes were at loose ends. They sat around talking awhile. The station was a big, self-contained building, with permanently sealed windows, and well insulated, and it was three o'clock before they woke up to the fact that there was something going on outside. They could see the tops of trees in the next block, from these upper-story windows, bending and shaking in all directions. Forbes went down to the lobby for a paper, and when he came back he said all hell was breaking loose out there. "There's a gale-force wind, must be blowing seventy miles an hour. We'll have some trees down if it keeps up."

"Damn," said Varallo, "I knew I should have got to cutting back those roses. They'll be blown to pieces."

Even in the well-insulated building, they could hear the wind roaring and howling. Katz came in dripping rain and shed his coat. "That's playing hell out there," he said, "we'll have some trees down."

"You been catching up to any more burglars?" asked Forbes lazily.

Katz laughed shortly. "We don't often get the breaks. No, damn it. There was a break-in at a big place up on Mountain— the people are away, they've gone back east to spend Christmas at a family reunion—the neighbors noticed the broken window and called in. It's a mess, of course—no telling what they got away with—but we found an address book, and the neighbors could tell us where they are. So now I run up the city's phone bill calling Massachusetts. Just in time to spoil their holiday. These damn punks—and the security was pretty good, but they got in, they always get in when they want to. At least if this storm keeps up, it should keep the punks home tonight."

O'Connor, Boswell, and Wallace came back, and O'Connor said crossly, "Nobody in his right mind is going to be hanging around the street in this. There's a great big tree down over on Broadway, blocking a whole lane."

It wasn't often they had a really rip-roaring storm in southern California, at least in the L.A. area, but this was going to be one of the times. Listening to the wind howling, they felt queerly insulated in the big, quiet building; but sooner or later they'd be going out to drive home. The clock dragged down to four-thirty, and Mary Champion came in, surveyed them and said, "Goofing off."

"No point in trying to do the legwork in this," said Forbes.

"You're not as dedicated to law and order as the honest citizens," said Mary amusedly. "I've got one in my office I think'll interest you, Charles."

"Oh?" said O'Connor.

She crooked a finger at him. "Come and see."

Downstairs in the Juvenile office, under Ben Guernsey's benevolent eye, a man was sitting in the chair beside Mary's desk, a tall, spare man with hatchet features. He was looking grim and angry. In the other chair was a boy about fifteen, and he'd been crying, was still hiccupping into a handkerchief. Mary said, "This is Lieutenant O'Connor, Mr. Bannister."

Bannister looked at O'Connor and said in a hard voice, "I brought him right in, as I was starting to tell these other officers. A kid of mine messing around with dope! I thought we'd taught him better sense. He comes home from school and when he takes off his coat, these damn things fall out of his pocket, and I think he's taken to smoking on the sly—I don't approve of that either but at least it's legal. It isn't until I see the look on his face and take another look at these damn things I realize it's dope—"

On Mary's desk were three more of the beautifully made marijuana cigarettes. "Ha!" said O'Connor pleasedly, and picked one up.

"You can smell it's not ordinary tobacco, it's marijuana, isn't it? I thought so. And I couldn't get anything out of this damn stupid kid, and all his mother can do is cry, but I fetched him right down to talk to you. Now, Rich, you're going to speak up loud and clear and tell the officers just where you got these damn things. And if I ever catch you with anything like this again, you're going to get the living tar whaled out of you."

"What about it, Rich?" asked O'Connor.

The boy shied back from his ferocious grin. He was sandy-haired, freckle-faced, an ordinary-looking kid. He mopped his face with the handkerchief and looked at his father with scared eyes. "Honest, Dad, I only smoked a couple joints before, some of the kids do all the time—they say it's nothing, doesn't do anything to you like the hard stuff, just sort of gives you a lift, like a drink, and most people drink liquor—"

Bannister said sharply, "You don't see your mother and me drinking liquor, do you? Where'd you get those things?"

The boy said miserably, sullenly, "From this guy. He's an older guy, like maybe in high school or college. His name's Bob. You meet him at a drugstore on the corner of Glendale Avenue and Chevy Chase, after school. Only a lot of the kids haven't got enough bread to buy from him, the joints he's got are two bucks each, but the kids all say they're worth it if you can get 'em because they're a lot better than most joints."

"Ha," said O'Connor again. "Did you buy these today?"

The boy shook his head. "Yesterday I got them. I hadn't smoked any of them yet, honest, today I just went right home, it was raining and blowing so hard."

Bannister said roughly, "And where the hell did you get the six bucks to buy them? You don't get that kind of allowance."

The boy was ready to cry again. "I saved up my lunch money. I don't need much lunch anyways."

"My God," said Bannister. "I thought you had some sense." He looked up at O'Connor. "Does this help you any, sir? If we could put these people out of business—seducing these stupid kids to get hooked on dope—"

"That's very damned useful, yes. Thanks very much, Mr. Bannister." He gave them a wolfish grin.

Bannister got up. "Come on, you." He hauled the boy to his feet. "Put on your coat, we're going home. I hope you realize how you've made your mother and me feel."

"I won't no more, honest, Dad—I—I knew it wasn't right, but it does make you feel sort of different and pretty good, I guess like a drink would. But I won't no more."

"You'd better not," said Bannister. "Come on. I just hope we make it home without getting blown off the road." He towed the boy out.

"And I doubt very much," said O'Connor, "that Bob will be plying his trade in this storm. We'll stake it out tomorrow and see if we can pick him up."

"And I hope the man's right," said Mary, "and we all get home without getting blown away. This is something."

It was something all right, when they went out into it. The

gale had increased and was a furious elemental power, whipping trees and bushes around savagely.

Varallo's Ford was a fairly heavy car, but on the way up to Hillcroft Road, he felt it shake and swerve as the wind hit it. He was thankful to get there, and locked the garage and dodged through the torrential rain into the service porch. The house felt warm and cozy; the noise of the wind lessened a little inside. "Thank goodness you got home," said Laura. "I was worried you might not make it, Vic. This is something, isn't it? Ginevra's been scared, and I think I've been too." The children came crowding up to be kissed, and Varallo took them down to the living room where there would usually have been a fire on the hearth. Gideon was crouched unhappily on the hearth rug. "Mommy put the fire out," said Ginevra. "She said about sparks in the chimney." That had been good thinking. Even in the rain the wind could carry sparks. Laura brought him a drink, and he sat down with Ginevra snuggled in his lap.

It took O'Connor half an hour to get home to Virginia Avenue; there was a tree down on Glenoaks, a big camphorwood, blocking three lanes, and no signs of a city crew out yet. The city crews would be busy cleaning up after this one. Katharine had been anxious, and she looked relieved to see him. "Thank goodness you got home. What a night! I hope it doesn't keep up long."

O'Connor kissed her. "Everything all right?"

"Oh, heavens, nothing could scare Vince, and Maisie hasn't got enough sense to be scared." Maisie was bouncing at him demanding attention.

"Whee!" said Vince exuberantly. "Whee! Blow everything away! Is it gonna blow the house down, Daddy?"

"I hope to God not," said O'Connor.

"How does it go—'Neither rain nor hail,' " said Harvey, " 'can stop us from our appointed rounds.' My God, this is the worst one we've had in years. Listen to that damn wind."

They had all got in a little late, and Rhys was worried about leaving his mother alone with the dogs. The dogs had been cowering under beds and tables, scared to death of the noise.

He went to look at the cat. The cat was serenely unworried, curled up asleep in her carton. There was an empty paper plate, an empty bowl, and a bowl of fresh water. Rhys went back to the big office and sat down. "I hope to God we don't get called out," he said. "Nobody'd be thinking of pulling off any jobs in this."

But of course they got a call ten minutes later. They all swore. It was an address on Rosedale Avenue, and it was a body. Rhys and Hunter took it. They leaned against the wind to reach the car in the parking lot, and on the way across town the wind buffeted the car unmercifully. The address was a well-maintained four-unit apartment, and the uniformed man was sheltering in a small, square entry hall. He said, "I didn't know if anybody'd turn out. You can hardly hold a car on the road."

"Where is it?" asked Rhys.

"Upstairs, the manager's there."

They went up shallow cement stairs to a landing between apartment doors. The man waiting for them there was short and stout, nearly bald; he was wearing old slacks and a sweater. He said, "What a night. But I had to report it, of course. I wish I'd got rid of the man long ago." He nodded at the door on the right; it was open. Rhys and Hunter went in. It was a pleasantly furnished living room, with a few personal touches: an oriental panel on one wall with a watercolor of birds and flowers, another over the mantel. Everything was clean and orderly; the only thing spoiling the looks of the place was the body of a man sprawled face down in the middle of the room. Rhys bent to look without touching him. His face wasn't visible, but he was a stocky man with dark hair, wearing a brown business suit. There was a little patch of dried blood behind one ear, and on the carpet beside him was a big wrench with dried blood showing on it.

"Not much of a mystery," said Hunter. "Let's hope there are some prints on that, Bob." They went back to the landing; the other man had stayed there. "What can you tell us about this, Mr.—"

"Davies," he said, "I'm James Davies. I manage the place, live downstairs."

"Who is he?" asked Rhys.

Davies was looking annoyed and disgusted. "His name's Calvin Ralston. I suppose he could have lain there for days, but I happened to remember he said the kitchen faucet was leaking, just the other day when he paid the rent, and I thought I'd come up and put a washer in—I do the little odd jobs like that. I was surprised when he didn't answer the door, I'd have expected him to be home. But I went back down and got my key, went in, and there he was. He's dead, I can see that."

"Did he live alone?" asked Rhys.

"Sure. I should have got rid of him, but hell, you live and let live, no? He was a quiet tenant, and my God, a lot of straight people can cause the disturbances with wild parties. You never heard a peep out of him. Sure, I knew he used to bring fellows here, but when he never gave any trouble, am I going to evict him with no real reason?" He shrugged.

"Oh," said Rhys. "He was a fag."

"That's right," said Davies. "You can't always tell them, but when he never had anybody here but other men—well, I know something about him. He's part owner of a hardware store on Broadway. He was always right on time with the rent. Live and let live, like I say."

"Hell," said Rhys. "Why didn't you wait till morning to find him?" But there was routine that had to be done. They called the lab from the squad, and Taggart came over in a van.

"Wild night," he said.

"Just get some pictures, Ray, so we can get rid of the body," said Rhys. "The other boys can have a better look tomorrow." They had already called the morgue wagon.

"Sure," said Taggart. It didn't take him long to get the necessary photographs and print the corpse. The morgue wagon arrived and the attendants carted the body off.

"We'll probably want to talk to you again, Mr. Davies," said Hunter.

"Anytime," said Davies.

They had got to the corner of Glenoaks and Pacific, on the way back to the station, when without warning every light in this part of the city went off. "Goddamn!" said Hunter. "The power's gone." In the dark the only lights left were automobile headlights. There wasn't a great deal of traffic, but it was difficult driving with all the streetlights gone and no traffic signals operating. They made it back to the station in half an hour, and were eminently thankful to see it looming up still ablaze with lights. The rain had slackened a little. At the rear door the big generator was roaring steadily away, providing power to the whole building and to the lights in the parking lot. It was warm and cozy up in the detective office.

Harvey said, "I just got the news on the radio. The whole north half of the city's out—lines down all over. This is the worst in years."

Rhys said, "By God, I'm not turning out again if somebody assassinates the mayor." He sat down at his desk and added, "There's not enough to put in a report on that yet. Leave it to the day watch."

Harvey said, "Anybody might have killed one like that," and suddenly every light in the building went out and left them in Stygian blackness.

"Goddamn it to hell," said Rhys, startled, "the damned generator's conked out!" He got up, took two steps, and ran violently into the next desk. "Is there a flashlight anywhere around?"

"Who knows?" said Hunter querulously out of the dark. They couldn't look in the dark. Harvey said, "It'll be hell down in Communications."

"The squads," said Rhys. He started to grope across the office toward the door. They were all familiar with the inside of the station, but darkness confused distances. He got out to the corridor, felt cautiously for the stairs, and nearly pitched down headfirst. He went down hanging on to the railing and, keeping one hand on the wall, groped his way down to the open door of Communications. It was chaos there. The switchboard operators, the people manning the radios, were getting calls, but they hadn't any way to take down information in the dark, and the girls were lamenting loudly, some of them scared. Rhys raised his voice. "Call up some of the squads, for God's sake! They'll have flashlights!" Nobody had thought of that yet, but the girls on the radios got busy.

In twenty minutes the first couple of squads rolled up. Rhys commandeered a flashlight from the first one and with its aid started down the basement stairs. The maintenance crew was supposed to keep a check on the generator, and they had a closet in the basement for supplies. There might be an emergency number. He thought angrily, I'll bet the stupid bastards forgot to check the diesel tank. He found the door and opened it. After flashing the light around a minute, to his relief he found a card tacked to the inside of the door with a number to call for emergency generator service. He scrawled it in his notebook, groped back to Communications and called it. There was a stream of calls coming in, mostly accidents.

They had to wait nearly an hour for the emergency service man, who'd had to come out from Pasadena and said it was hell driving. He went out with a flashlight and took the side panels off the generator. "The damn thing's out of oil," he said. "There's a safety shutoff for that. Goddamn it, that never entered my head, I haven't got any in the truck." He had to go back to his garage for eight quarts of oil, and it was another hour before he'd poured it in and the generator came thudding into life again and the station blossomed into blessed light.

Rhys went back upstairs thankfully and called his mother. She said, yes, the power was still off and the radio was saying nobody knew when it might come back on. "But everything's all right, Bob, I've got the kerosene lamps out."

"Yes, and I don't like those damn things. You be careful with them."

Toward dawn the wind suddenly died down, and when lights came on Wednesday morning, everything was still, the air very cold and clear. The city crews got the power back on at about seven A.M. The gray clouds had been swept away, and there was a sparkling view of all the snow on the back mountains. There had been a good deal of damage done all over town; trees were down and the streets full of debris.

When Delia came into the office, Varallo was already there talking to O'Connor and Gonzales. "Did you get any damage?" he asked her.

"No, not a bit—it's a pretty substantial house."

"They had an even wilder night here—Bob left a note. The generator went out, and it must have been hell in Communications until they got it working again. Damnation," said Varallo.

"I knew I should have cut back all the roses—I think I've lost half a dozen."

"We were lucky too," said O'Connor. "No damage, but the backyard's full of junk blown in."

"And we've got a new homicide," said Varallo.

"Well, you'll have to go and look at it with Gil," said Delia. "There are inquests scheduled on those Fullers and Jean Hoffman, somebody has to cover that."

"Hell and damnation," said Varallo, "I'd forgotten that. And those indictments—" Inevitably the court appearances came along, taking time from the regular daily work. The indictments were on a couple of heisters they'd dropped on three weeks ago, but that was a part of the routine too.

"And," said O'Connor sardonically, "the D.A.'s office wants a conference about Washburn. I gather they haven't decided whether to call it involuntary manslaughter or what."

Gonzales uttered a rude word. "I suppose I get that job. Have to drive clear downtown—at least it's not raining—and listen to those bleeding hearts throw around the legal double-talk."

"Well, there's also Bob with the pretty joints," said O'Connor. "And by the way, Vic, we're out of cat food." Varallo swore again.

He went out for the cat food, more Kitty Litter, and two more quarts of milk, and brought it back before he started out to do any work. Delia would be in court a good part of the day and Gonzales downtown at the D.A.'s office.

He landed at the apartment on Rosedale at ten o'clock and talked to the manager, Davies, awhile and looked over the apartment. Rhys had taken the manager's key last night, and the lab men would get here sometime today. There wasn't anything suggestive or helpful in the apartment except the bloody wrench.

The hardware store Ralston had partly owned was down on Broadway, a modest business enterprise, nothing classy. There he talked to the other owner, Boyd Hicks. Hicks was a younger man than Ralston, in his mid-thirties; he was red-haired and pugnacious. He took the news of Ralston's murder without much surprise or dismay. "The only thing is," he said, "where the hell does it leave me? I'll have to see a lawyer. I don't know what happens to the partnership. Listen, I didn't really know Ralston, if you get me. Sure, I knew he was a fag, but I didn't know it back when I advertised for somebody to help put up some money to start this business. I hardly ever saw him—once in a long while he'd come in to look over the books, is all."

"You aren't surprised about his getting murdered?"

"Listen," said Hicks cynically, "one like that, they're asking for it. You take some of the fags, they'll have a permanent pal, all nice and quiet, and they don't go asking for trouble. But Ralston lived alone, and I'd guess he went around picking up different ones. Asking for it. Sometimes those types can be hair-trigger. I'm not doing any grieving for him, if that's what you mean. But, goddamn, I wish I knew where I stood about the partnership." He added that he had the idea that Ralston was pretty well heeled, maybe other investments, he wouldn't know; but he hadn't held a job and was always dressed pretty sharp. He didn't, of course, know any of Ralston's pals.

There had been an address book at the apartment, where Burt and Thomsen would now be poking around for any scientific evidence. Varallo sat in the car and leafed through it. There weren't many names in it, and they were all first names—Lou, Jim, Gary, John—with just phone numbers appended. That might figure, but it was annoying. If Ralston had been the kind of fag who went around picking up casual one-night stands, almost anybody could have killed him, for any reason, and the killer wouldn't be listed in his address book. These were probably his more permanent pals, and possibly one of them had had a lover's spat with him, but he wouldn't admit it over the telephone. However, the police had certain privileges the ordinary citizen didn't. Varallo went back to the office and got hold of a supervisor at the local phone company, asked her to check out the addresses belonging to those phone numbers.

She said, "It may take a while, sir. I'll see what I can do." Correctly she had called him back to verify that she really was talking to the police.

"Whenever you can get to it," said Varallo. He couldn't say he was all that concerned or interested about who had used that wrench on Calvin Ralston.

At least, as Katz had said, the wild night had kept the burglars at home. And the heist men, and the muggers. But he hadn't yet caught up to the people visiting back in Massachusetts who'd had the burglar here. The family reunion seemed to be a movable feast, going from place to place.

Poor had gone to cover the arraignment of one they'd dropped on a couple of weeks ago. The office was empty. Katz got on the phone again, running up the city's bill, and finally this time got into contact with the householder, whose name was Fitton. He broke the news about the burglary and Fitton was agitated. "Goddamn it," he said, "we weren't coming home until after Christmas, but my God—"

"You understand, Mr. Fitton, we'd like to know exactly what's missing, and the house ought to be secured."

"Oh, my God!" said Fitton. "I don't know if I can get an airline reservation now—I can try—my God, if Martha's coin collection's gone she'll have a stroke—I'll let you know. Where should I call?" Katz gave him the number. "My God, and if I do get back home, I probably couldn't get another reservation back here—"

The burglar had spoiled all their Christmas plans, all right.

O'Connor had been hot to chase after Bob and the pretty joints, but he had got stymied. He got out to the drugstore by nine-thirty, but it was closed. By law there should have been an emergency number posted on the door, in case of fire or theft, but the card tacked up had been there so long it was indecipherable. Of course, it was very possible that the proprietor of the drugstore didn't know a damn thing about Bob, but it wasn't a big chain place, just a small independent drugstore. He went back to the office with Wallace. Boswell was in court covering an indictment.

The Bannister boy had said Bob was to be found there after school. At three o'clock O'Connor and Wallace got back there again, and by then the place was open.

The proprietor was a George Armitage. He was a fat man in the late sixties, with myopic eyes behind very thick glasses, and he said, "Well, sorry you missed me this morning, but we had some bad damage in the storm—part of the roof caved in—and I had to call a man in about it, arrange to have it fixed. Do I know a Bob? Which Bob you mean?"

"Maybe a young fellow about high school age."

"Oh, you wouldn't mean Bob Glessner? He's a nice, upstanding young fella, I like to see young people ambitious and hardworking like that. What in time could the police want with Bob?"

"You know him?"

"Surely I know him—known him for years, he lives somewhere around here, couldn't say where. I let him use the back alley behind the store—he came and asked—he's built himself up a nice little business, repairing bicycles, fixing up old ones to sell, for the younger kids. I let him keep the ones he's working on in the back room sometimes."

"Goddamn!" said O'Connor. "And isn't that a nice front!"

"Beg pardon?" said Armitage.

"We'd like to wait and see if he turns up," said Wallace.

"Oh, he won't be here today," said Armitage. "Not on Wednesdays. He's got a pretty heavy class schedule on Wednesdays, he told me."

"Where does he go to school?" demanded O'Connor loudly.

"What say? My wife says I'm getting a mite hard of hearing lately—oh, I couldn't say if he's still in high school or maybe goes to Glendale College."

By then, of course, the offices at all the schools were closed and there'd be no getting at the records. O'Connor growled and swore, and Wallace said soothingly, "We'll trace him tomorrow, Charles."

That night Katz's prediction came true.

It was Rhys's night off, Hunter and Harvey sitting on night watch alone. They hadn't got a call up to ten o'clock, and they were surprised and a little pleased when the cat emerged from O'Connor's office and strolled up asking for attention. "She looks fatter," said Harvey.

"That's the kittens, I guess. I don't mind a cat. Nice puss." The cat sat on Varallo's desk and purred.

They got the call at ten-thirty, to Justin Avenue. It was an old frame house, and the Traffic man was Weiss. He said, "It's these jokers again. The burglars who know the names. She's a Miss Lydia Brent, and she's pretty shook up."

She was a little woman in a pink bathrobe, with gray hair in a braid. She didn't look as old as some of the rest of the victims had been, but she was very pale and breathing shallowly. "Just take it easy, Miss Brent," said Harvey. "Tell us what happened."

"They said 'police'—you've got to trust the police," she said. "They rang the bell, and they said my name—a prowler in the backyard—I was just going to bed." She took a long gasping breath. "I was frightened—you see, my heart's not strong, I had a bad heart attack a couple of years ago and the doctor says—"

"Just relax and calm down, Miss Brent. Have you relatives we can call for you?"

"Oh, no, there's just my niece Linda—Linda Foley in Oregon. They came right in, and one of them had a knife—oh, dear, I do feel so queer—" And she toppled out of the chair to the floor.

Thirty seconds later Hunter said urgently, "We'd better call the paramedics, I can't find a pulse—" Harvey leaped to the phone. They were trying artificial respiration when the paramedics came and took her away in a hurry.

"Hell," said Harvey, "we'd better locate some keys and lock the place, in case another burglar—the day watch can take it from here—"

They started to look around, and Hunter said, "What the hell's that?" In the small dining room, most of the table was taken up by what might be a big packing case with an old blanket draped across it.

Harvey pulled the blanket loose, and looked, and said, "Well, for God's sake!"

CHAPTER 8

"I knew it!" said Katz passionately at nine o'clock on Thursday morning. He'd just put the phone down. "I said sooner or later this damn pair would scare one of these old people into a heart attack—so now it's your baby, Vic. This Miss Brent died last night. So I'll hand all the reports to you and you can take a ride on the merry-go-round. And I wish you joy of it." He sat back looking disgusted.

Varallo said, "Your mysterious burglars. Well, technically it is a homicide, but if we ever catch up with them, they wouldn't be charged with that."

"They damn well ought to be," said Katz. "This woman evidently had a bad heart condition, and when they broke in on her like that—it's a damn shame. You go and have fun with it. Maybe Delia's female intuition will turn up an idea."

"See if the lab picks up anything," said Varallo.

"Yes, we have to go through the motions. They haven't got anything for us on one of these jobs yet, but there could be a first time. On this one there's some relation, a niece in Oregon. Oh, and Jim left a note, there's a bird there, I suppose we better see it's taken care of, maybe one of the neighbors would take it until the niece gets here."

"We'll have to call her and break the news," said Delia. "Do you have the name?"

"Jim found the name and number in the address book at the house. It's a Linda Foley in Eugene, Oregon." He passed on the note. "I'll set the lab in motion just in case—Jim left the keys." He got up and went out, and Delia called the number in Oregon but didn't get any answer.

They all knew the gist of this one; Katz had done enough talking on it, and it was one of those simple little mysteries that could be baffling. How indeed could the burglars know all the names, so the old people would let them in so willingly? Apparently the only thing these people had had in common was their approximate age, all old people. She would try the Oregon number again later.

Varallo shared the gist of what he'd turned up on Ralston so far. "I did a little legwork on it yesterday and came up with damn all. All of these pals live right here in town, but I only found one of them, a Gary Adams. He's the drummer in a combo playing at a fancy bar in Toluca Lake. The other ones all live in cheap apartments, and nobody around seems to know where they work. Adams claims he doesn't know any of them."

"They pay rent somewhere," said Gonzales, "the landlord should know something about them."

"Yes, that's the next place to go. Delia can brood over Joe's little mystery for us."

They started out on the day's legwork, and Delia suddenly remembered Miss Brent's bird. A canary, she thought; maybe one of the neighbors would be willing to take care of it. She went out into the cold, clear air and drove over to Justin Avenue. The mobile lab van was parked in front, and as she went up to the front porch, Burt was just coming out. Delia said, "Joe said there was a bird."

"Oh, there's a bird!" said Burt bitterly. "*Is* there a bird!" He went past her and Delia went into the house. A long, loud wolf whistle greeted her and she jumped. Thomsen was dusting the coffee table. "That damn thing gives me the willies," he said.

What had looked like a packing case to Hunter and Harvey last night was a very large metal bird cage; it was about four feet high and three feet wide, and in the cage was a parrot. It was a large parrot and brilliantly colored; its whole head and back, including the wings, was a vivid bright royal blue, and its underbody down to its legs was an equally vivid orange. There were fine black lines on either side of its face above the great curved beak. "Hello, dear," said the parrot in a hoarse voice. "It's nice to see you home, dear, give us a little kiss!"

"For heaven's sake," said Delia.

"Yeah," said Thomsen.

Delia went up to the cage and the parrot said, "Yo-ho and a

bottle of rum!" There was a brass tag on the front of the cage; the engraving on it said *Henry*. "What a name for a parrot," said Delia. "Henry's a good boy, Henry wants an orange," said the parrot.

"Well, we'll have to do something about it, it's Miss Brent's property and I suppose the heirs will want it." Henry let out a loud screech and repeated the wolf whistle. "Let's all have a little drink! Scratch Henry's head, please!"

She tried the house on the right of Miss Brent's and faced a slovenly looking young woman who said they'd just moved in, didn't know any of the neighbors, and couldn't care less about one of them dying. She tried the house on the other side and introduced herself to a vague, middle-aged woman who said her name was Hughes. "I noticed people going and coming next door, is Miss Brent sick again?" Delia said she had died. "Oh, dear, that's awful. I'm sorry. But she hadn't been well in a long time, she had a bad heart. We didn't know her awfully well, but I do know that. She'd had to retire early, she was only about sixty, she'd been a schoolteacher all her life, but she had to retire a couple of years ago. I guess she was getting along all right, she had an annuity of some kind and her school pension."

"There's a parrot," began Delia, "we were wondering—Miss Brent's niece lives in Oregon and might not be able to come right away—if you could look after it until some arrangements—"

Mrs. Hughes recoiled. "That awful bird," she said. "Oh, no, I couldn't do that, I'm sorry. I understand Miss Brent's niece is married to a man with a lot of money. That bird—it belonged to Miss Brent's brother, she came by it when he died a couple of years ago. I don't like parrots, I couldn't take the responsibility, I'm afraid."

Delia went back to the Brent house and said to Thomsen, "No luck with the neighbors. Damn, we can't let the bird starve to death."

"Oh, my!" said Henry as if in alarm. "Oh, my! I like a little sugar in my tea. Give us a kiss, dear!"

"The pound," said Delia. "Maybe they'd look after it until the niece can come for it." The phone had been printed; she looked up the local Humane Society and dialed, but the phone rang emptily at her. "Damn," she said again. "There must be some-body there, to see to the animals. I suppose they're all out feeding them or something." The things like this cops came in for too. Public service, she thought, and got up. "It's nice to see you home, dear!" said Henry. "Did you have a nice day?" He had a very loud, hoarse voice.

Delia went out to the car and drove to the Humane Society on Ivy Street. It consisted of a rather small stucco building and a lot of cramped-looking outside runs. The front door was un-locked and she went in, but there wasn't anybody there. She went looking, past a large room where tiered cages held some cats, and a corridor door led her out to the side yard and the dog runs. Dogs yelped and barked plaintively, large and small dogs. There had to be such things as pounds, but— There was a lanky young man cleaning out one of the runs. Delia asked him if anybody else was there. "Oh, Mrs. Singer won't be in till about one," he said, "and both the Animal Control officers are up in the hills after coyotes." That might sound frivolous, but North Glendale had had problems with coyotes coming down from the foothills; the last couple of winters, a number of small pets had been killed and some children severely bitten. "Oh, I couldn't do anything about admittals, miss. You'd have to see Mrs. Singer, I'm just here to clean out the cages and do the feeding."

"Damn," said Delia. The things they had to do, wasting time. She went back to Justin Avenue. Thomsen was in the kitchen, Burt in the front bedroom. She said, "Look, Rex, when you're finished here you'd better bring the parrot cage back to the station."

"The station! That thing?"

"Well, it wouldn't fit in an ordinary car, and we can't let the parrot starve."

"It's nice to see you home dear, give us a little kiss!" said Henry loudly. "Yo-ho and a bottle of rum!"

"It's just until I can contact the pound," said Delia.

"My God," said Burt, "that thing's been driving us nuts. All right, but nobody's going to like it."

Delia looked at the cage. It was embellished with a perch and a suspended swing, mirrors and metal feeding dishes fastened to the inside. She had no idea what parrots ate, but Henry probably hadn't been fed since yesterday. She went out to the kitchen and looked in the cupboards. In the one to the right of the sink, she found a paper sack labeled *Dawson's Exotic Birds*. It was about a quarter full of some sort of seeds. She went back to the dining room and filled one of the dishes from outside the cage. Henry said uncannily, "Thank you, dear! Let's all have a little drink!" Delia laughed. There was something comically endearing in Henry's bright, beady eyes. He teetered on his perch and raised his bright blue wings.

Delia went back to the station and settled down over the sheaf of reports Katz had left on her desk.

When Burt and Thomsen got back at the station there didn't seem to be any out-of-the-way place to dump that great big cage, and they certainly didn't want it anywhere near the lab. They carried it down to the lobby and put it along the side wall. "What the hell?" said Sergeant Dick. "What's that?" Henry fluttered and gave a loud screech. "Hello, dear, give us a kiss!"

"You can't leave that damn thing here," said Dick, scandalized.

"It's just temporary," said Burt. "Property of a victim, and the detectives haven't contacted the relatives yet." Henry screeched again.

"My God," said Dick, "they'd better locate them damn quick."

O'Connor and Wallace had been on a little merry-go-round of their own. They'd tried Glendale High School first, but there wasn't any Bob Glessner in that student body. So they tried Hoover High and didn't find him there either. They went up to Glendale College and drew a blank.

There were eleven Glessners in the phone book, living in Glendale, all over town. But three of them were roughly in the right area, within thirty blocks of that drugstore, so they tried those first. There was nobody home at any of the places—two apartments and a single house—but they talked to a few neighbors. At the two apartments the neighbors could tell them that nobody named Bob Glessner lived there. At the single house, an old rundown place on Stanley Avenue, the neighbor said, yes, Bob Glessner lived next door. His parents were dead and he lived with his grandpa and grandma, and he went to Pasadena City College. So they drove over there and saw the principal, who was surprised.

"Glessner," he said. "I don't know all our students individually, it's a very large student body, but I happen to know Bob Glessner because I'm a chess player myself—he's the president of our chess club, a very bright young man indeed. Why should the police be interested in Glessner?" He looked doubtfully at O'Connor's stocky bulk, the bulge of the .357 magnum.

O'Connor asked, "Will he be in class somewhere now?"

"Probably—I can look up his schedule for you." By the time he'd done that, it was just noon, and they found Bob Glessner coming out of his French class. He was a tall, strikingly good-looking dark fellow about twenty-one, and he was polite, but his eyes flickered at the badges.

"What do the cops want with me?" he asked pleasantly.

"We think you've built up a nice little business for yourself, Bob, but not repairing the bicycles. The pretty little joints. And very pretty they are."

"I don't know what you mean," he said.

Wallace said, "Oh yes, you do." There were students crowding the corridors and it was noisy. They led him out of the building. "Do you have a car?"

He didn't answer for a minute and then just nodded. "So all right, let's go look at it," said O'Connor. He took Glessner by one arm. "You might as well show us, we'd find it anyway."

In stiff silence Glessner walked across the campus to the parking lot and up to an old Pontiac sedan. Wallace hung onto his arm while O'Connor went over the car; Glessner produced the keys without a word. The merchandise wasn't concealed; in a carton on the floor of the backseat were about a hundred of the well-made joints, neatly packed away.

"So," said O'Connor genially, beaming at him, "suppose you tell us where these came from. And don't ask us to believe they were a present from Santa Claus."

"Damn," said Glessner. "The old man's going to be mad as hell, but I can't help that."

"You've been peddling these things quite a while, haven't you?" asked Wallace. "Where do you get them?"

Glessner said, "The old man. My grandfather."

"Now look," said O'Connor dangerously, "don't try to spin us any goddamn yarn like that—"

"No," said Glessner, "that's straight. You'll find out now anyway. The old man makes them, him and my grandmother. It was his idea. He grows the stuff in the backyard and makes the joints himself. He got the idea when prices started to go so high. They've just got the Social Security, and he figured it was a good way to make something on the side. He's going to be mad as hell about this. I've just been selling them for him is all."

For once O'Connor was at a loss for words. Then he said, "So let's go back to Glendale." Wallace drove the Pontiac with Glessner sitting silently beside him, and O'Connor trailed them back to Stanley Avenue. It was a block of tired old houses, but the lots were standard size, fifty by a hundred and fifty. Now there was a car in the drive, a battered-looking two-door Ford. Glessner went up the front walk with them and opened the front door. In a shabbily furnished living room, an old man was sitting watching a black and white TV. Glessner went over and shut it off. "I'm sorry as hell, Gramps, but the cops have found out. I had to tell them, they'd have got us anyway."

The old man stood up and looked at them. He was a tall, lank, bald old man with sharp features, a narrow mouth like a trap. He said, "Goddamn it, Bob, I always told you to be careful, you give it away someways, damn it—"

"No, I didn't, Gramps, somebody must have snitched. You know the kids got more sense than to do that—" He looked at O'Connor. "Who did snitch?"

"You misjudged one new customer, Bob, he wasn't quite roped and tied yet," said O'Connor pleasurably. He looked at the old man. "Let's have your name."

"Weston J. Glessner," he said sullenly. "Damn it, we had to do something, with money so damned tight. So what if it ain't legal, they got so damn many laws in now there's hardly any damn thing is legal, and I don't reckon that stuff's no different from tobacco, I been smoking tobacco since I'm fifteen and it's never did me no harm. Oh, hell, I'd make you get a warrant but you'd just come back again."

O'Connor went out to look at the backyard. At the rear of it, in a plot about forty feet square, was a lush crop of marijuana. It was a very pretty plant, with shiny green leaves. When he went back into the house, an old woman had joined the other two, a wrinkled little old lady in a cotton housedress, and she was saying mournfully, "It's just an awful shame, boys, after we all put in so much work on it, just to be independent and look after our own needs—that last batch came out real nice—"

They found a professional-looking drying oven in the kitchen, full of newly gathered leaves being processed, and a cigarette-making machine in the old couple's bedroom. "You've got quite a professional setup here," said O'Connor. "You've been turning out some nice joints, Glessner."

He gave a little cackle of a laugh. "One of the first jobs I ever had, back when I was fourteen or fifteen, was runnin' a cigarette-making machine—back in West Virginia. I always was neat-fingered. I'm just sorry as hell you found out about it. It's been bringin' in a mighty nice profit."

The old woman said indignantly, "Cops always comin' around interfering! Spoil the whole business, after we got it going real good! All we wanted was to take care of our own needs, be independent—I don't hold with charity. And the Social Security just don't go very far."

Delia went out to lunch with Mary Champion, but she was abstracted. She'd been going through all of Katz's reports, and she was seeing clearer what he'd been talking about, what a funny little mystery it was. After the first three or four cases, Katz had really done the spadework, finding out everything about these people, digging for any possible connection among all the victims, looking for any possible way that the burglars could have known all those names. And there just wasn't any. There was absolutely no connection at all; the victims hadn't known each other or shared any even vague affiliations. Beyond the fact that they were all elderly, and all of them drawing Social Security, there was just nothing. And Social Security checks, bearing the names, were issued in Washington, D.C.

"I've asked you twice," said Mary tartly, "how long you're going to leave that damn bird in the lobby. It's been driving us nutty." The Juvenile office was right across from the lobby.

"I'll try to get the Humane Society again after lunch," said Delia meekly.

But first she tried again to get the niece in Oregon, and this time got an answer but not a very satisfactory one. The voice at the other end said, "Oh, I'm just the house sitter, the Foleys are away. They won't be back until Monday. They're on a vacation in Hawaii. I'm their cleaning lady, they hired me to stay in the house in case of burglars, and look after the cat." Hearing about Miss Brent, she said, "That's too bad, I'm sorry, I know Mrs. Foley thought a lot of her aunt. But I don't know where you could reach her, they went with another couple who own a condominium there and I don't know their name."

Delia put the phone down and said, "Damn." She reached for it to try the Humane Society again, and it shrilled at her.

"Say, listen," said Sergeant Dick, "when the hell are you going to get this bird out of here? It's driving me nuts. It keeps asking me to have a drink and calling me dearie. I've had a couple of citizens in, and it looks funny—undignified, sort of. I don't know why the hell anybody wants a parrot."

Delia said, "I'm working on it, Bill." She called the Humane Society, but there still wasn't anybody there.

The phone rang again and it was Burt. "Say, we picked up some good latents on that wrench at Ralston's apartment yesterday, I'm just sending a report up to Varallo. I ran them through R. and I. and they haven't got them, so I sent them back to the Feds just now. We should get a kickback sometime."

"Fine," said Delia. She went down to the lobby to look at Henry.

"Driving me nuts," said Sergeant Dick.

Henry seemed to be excited and interested at his change of scene. He was teetering back and forth on his perch and ruffling his bright blue wings. "Hello, dear," he said. "Henry's a good boy! Henry wants an orange! Let's all have a little drink!"

"Can't you get the pound to take it?" asked Dick.

"I can't reach anybody there with any sense," said Delia crossly. She wondered if there was a Humane Society in Burbank. If so, it would probably be an even smaller operation than the one here. And she had a further thought, while Henry emitted a series of wolf whistles. Yes, get the Humane Society to take Henry, just to take care of him until the niece arrived; and there might be a mix-up—they didn't seem to be very efficient —and Henry might end up destroyed along with the other unwanted creatures, and the niece would sue the Glendale Police Department for losing valuable property. Delia had the vague idea that these exotic birds were quite valuable.

"Yo-ho and a bottle of rum!" said Henry. "I like a little sugar in my tea. Hello, dear, it's nice to see you home!"

Delia went upstairs again moodily. Nobody else was in. She reread some of those reports, and if she possessed any female intuition, it wasn't telling her anything. She wondered where everybody was. If the prints on that wrench were identifiable, it was a waste of time for Varallo and Gonzales to be out doing the legwork, beating the bushes for Ralston's little pals.

She was still sitting there smoking too much at three-thirty when a new call went down. Surprisingly it was to Buffums' Department Store over in the Galleria. They wouldn't be calling out detectives for a shoplifter. She went downstairs, belting her coat, and at the bottom of the staircase, as she turned into the rear hall, she heard Henry from the lobby. "Awk!" said Henry in a long screech, and let out his wolf whistle. "Did you have a nice day, dear? Scratch Henry's head! Give us a little kiss!"

If she couldn't get the Humane Society to take Henry, something would have to be done. He'd have to be fed again eventually, and the cage cleaned out.

Over in the enormous shopping plaza, Buffums' occupied a prominent position at one end of the mall, a three-story building standing alone. It was a very good department store, with quality merchandise. There were two squads and an ambulance illegally parked in front, but as she approached the wide front doors the ambulance pulled away. One of the uniformed men was waiting for her just inside the doors; it was Tracy.

"This is a little thing," he said. "A hell of a place for you to do anything, and I don't know what you can do at that."

"What is it?" asked Delia.

"Well, this woman got pushed down the escalator, and she's dead. When I got here, first I called an ambulance and then I saw she was dead—probably she fractured her skull or something like that, it was the down escalator and you know those steps are pretty sharp-edged the way they turn up. And my God, talk about preserving the scene, there's no scene to preserve. With a thousand Christmas shoppers milling around—I called a backup and called you."

"Why?" asked Delia. "If she just fell down the escalator—"

"No, she was deliberately pushed, we've got a witness." He led her in. It was something of a madhouse, of course, a big department store at this time of year. There were crowds surging all over this ground floor. There was an enormous and very beautiful Christmas tree, all white and gold, rising forty feet just inside the front door, and soft, piped-in Christmas music playing in the background all over the store. At the left of the tree, fifty or sixty feet from the doors, were the escalators, side by side, and there was a little huddle of people there, all men, with the other Traffic man.

"I didn't know what to do," said Tracy. "All these people—but after Moore got here, I roped in a couple of the clerks in the menswear department, the manager was here then and the store detective, and they've kept people away—that was after the girl came down and told us she'd been pushed—"

At one side of the bottom of the down escalator was the body of a woman face down on the floor. There was a handbag, its handle still caught around her right arm, and a couple of packages, big paper bags with the Buffums' logo on them. She was a medium-sized woman with dark hair, wearing a black wool coat and black shoes with sensible low heels.

"Mr. Fellows saw her come down," said Tracy. "This is Detective Riordan, sir, you just tell her what you told me."

He was a short, plump man with a blond mustache, and he was still a little excited. "It was a terrible thing—of course, I didn't know then she was dead. I'm in menswear right over there. I saw her all sprawled out on the escalator as it came down, and I thought she'd fallen. I came over—there wasn't anybody above her on the escalator, that was pure chance because usually there'd be a dozen people on both escalators—and she sort of slid off it, you know, as it came to the ground floor, and I was afraid her clothes might get caught in the machinery, I came to help her up. And she was unconscious. I thought she'd fainted, I called Mr. Braun—he's one of the store detectives, he was over by the door—"

"Me," said the big red-faced man beside him. "So did I, you can have accidents on escalators, and people suing the store. But we couldn't bring her to, and after about five minutes I couldn't feel a pulse at all, and I called upstairs to the office and Mr. DePugh came down."

He was the third man in the group. He introduced himself as one of the store managers. "We've never had such a thing happen before," and he sounded more annoyed than sorrowful. "And at the busiest time of the year—but when I heard what Mrs. Sanders had to say, I realized it was a matter for the police. We still didn't realize she was dead then."

"Mrs. Sanders," said Delia.

"She's upstairs in scarves and gloves, she told us the woman was pushed. She says it was quite deliberate."

Delia looked at the crowds, at the body. There wasn't much scope here for any lab work, and it probably wasn't necessary. She knelt beside the body and disentangled the bag from the woman's arm. It was a commodious black leather bag with several compartments. In the first one was a tan billfold. She opened it. The first plastic slot held a driver's license for Ellen Lambert, forty-six, five-five, brown hair and blue eyes, an address on Grandview Avenue in town.

She said to Tracy, "You'd better take the bag and packages to the station when you get back." It was the end of the Traffic shift now. "Call the morgue wagon and stand by till it comes. Where do I find Mrs. Sanders?"

DePugh said mechanically, "Scarves and gloves on the second floor." He mopped his brow. "We've never had such a thing happen before. And really I don't see any way the store can be assumed to be responsible—"

All this while the crowds had been passing, mostly women casting curious and alarmed looks at the body and the little group of people around it; but nobody was disposed to linger—

an accident, someone taken ill, someone fainted: someone official would see to it, pass by and don't look.

"OK," said Tracy. "I guess it's the only thing to do."

Delia put the billfold in her own bag and went over to the up escalator. If there was any blood on one of those sharp-edged stairs endlessly appearing and reappearing on the down escalator, it was long gone and probably didn't matter. At the top of this escalator, on the second floor, she stepped off and looked around. Across the aisle from the escalator was a four-sided showcase displaying scarves, gloves, some knitted hats. She went over there. "Mrs. Sanders?" She brought out the badge.

There was only one clerk behind the counter, a young woman with shoulder-length chestnut hair, a good, slim figure in a beige knitted dress. She looked at the badge and said, "Are you a detective? I thought it'd be another man—the cop said a detective would want to talk to me. She was a big fat woman in a bright pink raincoat, she had white hair."

"Who?" asked Delia.

"Didn't the cop tell you? The one who pushed her. I saw the whole thing, it was awful. She was a lot bigger than the other woman, and I guess she must have caught her off balance, she was just going to step onto the escalator."

"All right, let's hear exactly what happened," said Delia patiently.

"Well, I didn't have any customers right then, this isn't as busy a department as some, and I was just standing here. You can see that I'm looking right across toward the escalators. And just then the aisle wasn't crowded either—people sort of come by in batches, you know. And so I saw the whole thing. The first woman, the smaller one, went to the down escalator, she came from the direction of the front of the store—and the other one seemed to be sort of chasing her, she took her by the arm and said something to her—"

"You couldn't hear what?"

Mrs. Sanders shook her head. "It was too far away, and the music and all the other noise—but she was talking to her, and she looked mad. I could just see her from the side, you know—not full face—but you could tell she was mad. She sort of shook the other woman by the arm. The other woman didn't do any talking at all, she just pulled her arm away and stepped over to get on the down escalator. And that's when the big woman shoved her. She gave her a real hard push, and like I say, maybe she caught her off balance, and I saw her fall—start to fall, she went right down headfirst—and I thought, golly, she could get hurt real bad, that was an awful thing to do—and I came out from behind the counter and went to look."

"What happened to the other woman?"

"I don't know. I didn't notice—I sort of got the feeling she just walked away down the aisle. I was just interested in the other one—I looked down the escalator, there were people in front of that woman, but I don't think any of them noticed her fall, they'd be facing the other way, of course. She was all sprawled out, head down—and I thought, golly, I'll bet she's really hurt bad and somebody ought to hear how it happened. So I went down—and one of the clerks in menswear was just bending over her, sort of pulling her off the escalator—and then Mr. Braun came up. And I told them what had happened, and then Mr. DePugh came and said they'd better call the cops and probably they'd want to hear what I had to say. And that first cop said the detective would want to talk to me."

"Would you recognize the woman if you saw her again?"

"Say, would I! A great big fat woman with white hair in kind of a poodle cut, and that bright pink raincoat. She had a double chin and a kind of hooked nose."

Delia thought about that for the space of one minute, and then she said, "We'd like a formal statement about this, Mrs. Sanders. Could you come to the police station in the morning to make one?"

Mrs. Sanders said readily, "Sure, I'm not on until noon. Is that poor woman dead? Mr. DePugh said he thought she was. Golly, that's awful. He chased me right back up here, not to miss any customers. Sure, I'll be glad to do that."

"Fine. Are there any public phones here?"

"Sure, downstairs the other side of cosmetics."

Delia found a phone and called in. She got Varallo, who'd just landed back at the office, and outlined the situation crisply. "It's just a chance, and it'll mean some overtime. But the woman sounds like somebody you'd notice, and if she'd been shopping in here, and bought something, a clerk might remember her. Of course, if she bought something and paid cash for it, forget it. But a lot of people use credit cards."

"Yes," said Varallo. "I see that—if she did, there'd be some way to trace her. But that's the hell of a big store, Delia."

"Yes, and we've got to cover every department in it before closing time. Because all the clerks are a lot busier than usual, the crowds of shoppers out, and if one of them did wait on her today, he or she might not remember it by tomorrow. I could use a little help, and we won't get dinner for a while."

"Yes," said Varallo.

"But somebody ought to call the Lambert woman's home and break the news." She passed on the address.

"Yes," said Varallo again. "It's getting on for five. I'll see if I can raise somebody. I seem to be the only one in, Gil hasn't come back yet and Charles just looked in a while ago to apply for some warrants. He was looking pleased with himself about something. All right, I'll be over eventually, let's say we meet at the front door at six and we'll coordinate the hunt."

"Good. Have you met Henry yet?"

"Henry who?"

"Go out by the lobby and see," said Delia. "I'm afraid Henry's going to be a little problem."

When Varallo came through the electric-eye doors, spotted her, and came over to join her, he said, "I see what you mean about Henry. Dick's wild about it. I will say, Henry's a good talker, isn't he? I hope to God you can contact the Humane Society tomorrow."

They divided it up by floors, Varallo to take all the departments on the ground floor, Delia those on the second. The woman might have bought anything anywhere in the store, if she'd been shopping here at all. The store would be closing at nine.

The started out on the job immediately; it was, as Varallo said, a big store. Delia began methodically at the rear of the second floor in women's coats, and of course it took time, she couldn't interrupt sales and had to wait to get the clerks' attention before asking, "Do you recall waiting on a woman who looked like this," and describing the fat woman and her pink raincoat. She worked her way through women's better dresses, suits, lingerie, nightwear, children's wear and infants' clothing, and at eight-thirty was talking to the clerks in linens and white goods at the front of the store when a discreet soft bell began to sound alerting late customers that the store was closing. She had drawn a blank talking to the last clerk there, and they were clearing out the cash register; the last few customers were departing. Resignedly she started for the escalators, and spotted Varallo's tall figure with its crest of blond hair just stepping off the up escalator. He took her arm and said, "I've got her—but we'll have to be snappy, they're just closing." He guided her onto the down escalator in a hurry. "I thought you'd like to hear chapter and verse. It was the cosmetics department, she remembered her right away."

They rode down; the cosmetics counter was just up from the front double doors of the store. The clerk was a thin blond girl with unexpectedly shrewd blue eyes; she was obviously impatient to get away, looking at her wristwatch. Here on the ground floor apparently all the last customers had been shooed out; a few uniformed security guards were wandering around.

The clerk said, "Look, we're closing—yeah, I just told this guy, I remember that woman. Big fat woman in a bright pink raincoat. One reason I remember, it was just before my break, I'm due for a break at two-fifteen and I was dying for a cup of coffee—look, it's after nine, we're closing—"

"Do you remember how she paid you?" asked Delia. "Did she use a credit card, a store account?"

"No, and usually I wouldn't remember about that either, with a couple of hundred customers a day, how would I? But it was the time, see, my break—all I was thinking about was a cup of coffee and sitting down for a while, but I had to finish waiting on her, naturally. I think it was some cologne she got, and something else, dusting powder or something—and I thought, brother, if it's a credit card, it'll hold me up another five or ten minutes—the number has to go up to the computer, you know, in case there's a stop on the card. But she gave me a check, so that didn't take much time."

"You don't remember her name?"

"Gee, no, I didn't take any notice of that. On a check you just ask for a driver's license, put down the number, and a credit card, take that number."

"And what happens to the checks?" asked Varallo.

"Well, everything goes upstairs—the security guard's just been to get the bag here. All the cash and checks, the guards come on just before closing and take everything up to Accounting, to the business office on the top floor."

"Damn," said Varallo mildly. But as they both saw, it was six of one and a half dozen of the other. If they'd found this clerk half an hour earlier, that check would have still been in her cash register; they would have had to get official permission to commandeer all the checks in that register, but of course there wouldn't have been that many personal checks in the register of only one department. As it was—

"Damn," said Varallo again. They went out the front door of the store and stood there a moment; departing clerks jostled past them.

"The business office is closed now, of course," said Delia. "I wonder how many checks the store takes in on an average per day. Because we're going to have to look at every single one of them. And most of them will have been signed by women. And we won't know which is which. Nothing to say which department in the store took them."

"And get the addresses from the checks, and then go and look at all those women to find the big fat woman with white hair. There's the DMV," said Varallo doubtfully.

"Don't quibble, Vic." They could ask the DMV in Sacramento for photostats of those drivers' licenses, having the numbers; a general physical description appeared on all drivers' licenses. But it would be an unusual request, and like any government department, the DMV would take its own sweet time; that might take weeks.

"Well, sometimes it comes down to the simple legwork. And I'm starving."

"So am I," said Delia. It was a quarter past nine. "Get here first thing in the morning and get hold of those checks before the accounting department sends them to the bank."

"Let's go and see if Laura can rustle up a scratch dinner."

Rhys came in a few minutes late. As he went down the hall to the front of the stairs, he was startled to hear a voice from the lobby and went to look. There was nobody on the desk at night —everything was routed through Communications—and there was just a dim muted light in the lobby.

"Hello, dear. Henry's a good boy. Scratch Henry's head! Did you have a nice day, dear?" Henry was teetering on his perch, ruffling his wings. "Henry wants an orange," he said plaintively.

"And where the hell did you come from?" said Rhys. He went on upstairs.

Hunter and Harvey could tell him where Henry came from, of course. "But why bring the damn thing here, I don't know," said Harvey. "Oh, the niece lives in Oregon, I suppose she couldn't come right away, but I should think the day watch could have left it with a neighbor or something."

Rhys went to check on Mama cat, who was peacefully asleep in her carton. There were about ten new cans of cat food lined up on top of the file case in O'Connor's office and a fresh sack of Kitty Litter in one corner.

They got a call at ten-forty, an attempted rape at a small shopping square, the Glendale Fashion Center up on Glendale Avenue. All the stores there would have been closed by nine o'clock, but all sorts of things happened in all sorts of places, and Rhys and Harvey went out to see what this one was philosophically.

It was a Mrs. Glenda Watson. She was somewhere in her forties, a gruff-voiced blonde, and she said, "I just thought you ought to know there's a creep like that roaming around here. I'd stayed late to work on the books—" She owned a dress shop here, Glenda's Modern Fashions. "And when I came out to the car he tried to jump me. He was talking dirty, I won't bore you with the details, but I wasn't about to be raped at this late date —I've gone through two husbands and the whole damn thing's a bore—so I just gave him a good hard kick where it'd do the most good, and he folded and I came back to the store and called you. Oh, I couldn't give you any description, it was dark out there. Just a creep."

When they got back to the office, Henry was still muttering

away in the lobby and Rhys went in there. "Henry wants an orange! Henry's a good boy! Scratch Henry's head! Yo-ho and a bottle of rum. Aaawk!"

Rhys wondered uneasily if the poor thing was hungry. He supposed they'd have to take care of it until Miss Brent's niece got here.

CHAPTER 9

Varallo was off on Friday. Delia and Gonzales were waiting at the front door when Buffums' opened at nine o'clock, and they talked to the chief of the accounting department, whose name was Chaffin. He listened to the story and said, "Well, you're in time, but just. All those checks would be sent to the banks this morning. Of course you want all of them?"

"Yes," said Delia, and he sighed.

"It'll take a while to collect them all right."

Gonzales asked, "Is there any way to tell which department took them in?" Chaffin shook his head. That would just make it a longer job. Chaffin went out of his little cubicle of an office and talked to a couple of other men in the hall. Delia and Gonzales waited for quite a while. It was after ten o'clock when Chaffin came back with a good-sized carton and handed it over. "You understand we'll have to have them back?"

"We're just after the names and addresses," said Gonzales. "You'll probably get them back in a couple of days."

On the way back to the office, Delia said, "And of course I get the job of making up the list. You'd better call the Lambert woman's sister." Varallo hadn't been able to raise anybody at the Grandview address last night, had gone over there to find it was an apartment, and had talked to the manager. Ellen Lambert had been a divorcée living alone, had worked the night shift at the phone company, and the manager thought her only relative was a sister in Indianapolis.

When they came into the detective office, Gonzales said, "Well, look who's back with us." Rosie was sitting on the floor beside Boswell's desk.

"Oh no," said Delia. This time it was obvious how Rosie had escaped from home. There was an eight-inch link of thin, stout cord attached to her collar, and it had been neatly chewed in half. "She was waiting at the front door when I went down to get a paper," said Boswell. "This is getting to be monotonous." Rosie grinned at him and he bent to pat her. "Another job for you, Delia—try to get hold of that Mrs. Beal."

Delia had to look up the number, but nobody answered. Gonzales and Forbes went out on the perennial legwork, and only Poor was in, typing a report. It was Katz's day off.

There was quite a sizable stack of checks in the carton. Delia uncovered her typewriter and set about the tedious job resignedly, and of course it took some time. Most of the checks had been signed by women, as she had deduced, but on some of the signatures it took a little deciphering to be sure of that, when the checks were on joint accounts. There were over a hundred checks, and eighty-seven of them had been signed by women.

She was interrupted in the job when Mrs. Sanders came in to make a statement. That took three quarters of an hour. She hadn't got halfway through the list of names by lunchtime. Then she tried to call Mrs. Beal, but she still wasn't home. Delia went out to lunch and then drove down to Ivy Street. This time she found Mrs. Singer in the office of the Humane Society and explained their problem about Henry. Mrs. Singer, a sallow-faced woman with untidy dark hair, nearly recoiled. "A parrot —oh, we haven't any facilities for taking care of birds, I'm afraid."

Delia said, "It would only be for a few days."

"Oh, no," said Mrs. Singer definitely, "I'm afraid we couldn't accept the responsibility. When there's a known owner to take it—" Quite obviously she didn't have the imagination to envision Henry disrupting the police station. Delia sat in the car and thought. Miss Brent's niece would be home on Monday. Only three days. But in the meantime— She found a public phone and looked in the yellow pages, remembering the name on the paper bag. *Dawson's Exotic Birds* was on South Brand. She found a parking space a block away and walked back.

The storefront was plastered all over with signs—Sale, Going Out of Business. Behind a counter displaying toys for parakeets, a cheerful-looking blond man listened to her problem and said, "Well, they're not difficult to take care of, what kind of parrot is it?" Delia described Henry. "Oh," he said, "what you've got there is a yellow and blue macaw, they're nice birds."

"We thought it was a parrot," said Delia.

"It is a parrot, they're all parrots—parrotlets, parakeets, cockatiels, macaws—just different varieties. That macaw is one of the friendliest and most affectionate ones, and a great talker. Well, they eat seeds and nuts—sunflower seeds—any soft fruit, all greens—if you can get the branches from a fruit tree, lemon or orange, they'll appreciate the whole branch. They should have water, of course."

"I see," said Delia. "I don't suppose you'd be inclined to look after it until the woman—"

"Oh, I'm afraid not. I'm closing out the business here, it's a rotten location, I'm going in with my brother out in Sherman Oaks."

Delia bought a large package of sunflower seeds. Then she found Ellen Lambert's address on Grandview Avenue and talked to the apartment manager. "I didn't know her very well," said the manager. "She'd lived here about a year, but I didn't see much of her. I do know she had a sister in Indianapolis." She let Delia into the apartment upstairs. It was a pleasant apartment, nicely furnished. There was an address book in the top drawer of a small desk, and under the *E*'s she found an address and phone number for Claire Ervin in Indianapolis. She sat down at the desk where the phone was and dialed the number. Claire Ervin had a pleasant contralto voice. Delia broke the news to her and she began to cry, but kept her head and tried to be sensible. "I just don't know what to do—and so near Christmas—I don't know a soul out there, and Ellen didn't have any close friends there—she wanted to get away from here after she and John got divorced, I said it was a mistake to go so far off—"

"Would you want the body sent back there? I could give you the name of a funeral director here, they could make the arrangements."

"Oh, dear," said Mrs. Ervin. "Maybe that's the best thing to do, yes—and now I'll have to tell Mother—" She was crying again. Delia gave her the name and address of a local funeral director. It was two-thirty when she got back to the office; she'd stopped at a market to get half a dozen oranges and a small head of lettuce for Henry. In the lobby Sergeant Dick was talking to a citizen at the desk. "We don't have those forms here, sir, you'll have to go to the courthouse—" The citizen was staring fascinated at Henry in the enormous cage.

Henry was restless. He was bouncing up and down on his perch and muttering to himself, letting out screeches and wolf whistles. "Henry wants an orange—scratch Henry's head!" Delia filled one feed dish with sunflower seeds and borrowed Dick's knife to peal and cut up the orange. The citizen had gone out. "Listen," said Dick.

"We have to take care of it," said Delia. "You can wash the knife, Bill." She got a *Times* off the rack and gingerly opened the cage door, but Henry was preoccupied with the orange and didn't make any attempt to get out. He was balancing on one foot, holding a piece of orange in the other and sucking it voraciously. She wadded up the old newspapers lining the cage and put in the clean papers. "Thank you, dear!" said Henry uncannily. "Yo-ho and a bottle of rum! You're a very pretty girl, dear!" Delia took the old papers out to the trash bin in the alley behind the station.

Dick said, "If that bird's here much longer—"

When she came into the detective office, O'Connor was there talking to Boswell and Wallace, and Rosie was curled up under Boswell's desk. "Heavens," said Delia. "Isn't Mrs. Beal home yet?"

"I just tried to call her again," said Wallace. "There's nobody there. The little dog's no trouble, she just seems happy to be here. I'll try the woman a little later."

Delia went back to making up the list of names from the checks; she wasn't halfway through yet.

At twelve-thirty Leo Boswell finished typing a report. Rosie was lying under his desk, and he suddenly realized that she'd been in here quite a while. He hoped she was housebroken. He got up and said, "Come on, Rosie," and took her down to the back door. She pattered after him obediently. He didn't have a leash for her, but she was a friendly little dog and he figured she'd come when he called her. He let her out, and Rosie apparently divined his intention; she trotted up to the bushes by the entrance to the driveway, accomplished her errand at once, and ambled back to him. "Well, you're a smart one, aren't you?" said Boswell. "Now, we're all going out for lunch, but we'll be back pretty soon."

Chief of Police Jensen, like everybody else at the station, usually came and went by the rear door, from the parking lot. His office was in a quiet niche at the back of the building. But today he'd been asked to give an informal talk to a lunch meeting of the Lions Club, and one of the Lions had picked him up in the parking lot and driven him up to Pikes' Verdugo Oaks Restaurant. The meeting had been very successful, the speech had gone over well, and the Lions had been cordial and kept him on with interested questions. It was nearly three-thirty when he was dropped off at the front door of the station, and he was feeling pleased with himself and life in general. He went in the double doors and was immediately greeted by a loud wolf whistle. He whirled and stared. "Hello, dear, it's nice to see you home! Did you have a nice day? Give us a little kiss! You're a very pretty girl, dear! Let's all have a little drink!"

The chief gave one look at the enormous cage and was transfixed by Henry's black, beady eyes. "Sergeant, just what in the name of God and all His angels is this damned bird doing here?"

"Well, that's just what I said, sir," said Sergeant Dick. "It's driving me bats, and it doesn't look right—undignified, like I told Miss Riordan. It's the property of a homicide victim, I gather, and the detectives haven't located the relatives yet."

Henry bounced on his perch and uttered a wolf whistle. "Undignified!" said the chief. He marched upstairs and made for the detective office. O'Connor was just going into his office past the door of the bigger room. "O'Connor!" said the chief, and then his eye fell on Rosie, who was having her ears scratched by Wallace. The chief followed O'Connor into the office. "Just what the hell are you running here, O'Connor, a menagerie? This is a police station, not a zoo! I—" He stopped in mid word. He'd just met the gaze of the gray tabby cat, who was sitting on O'Connor's desk blotter looking at him interestedly. "For the love of God!" said the chief forcefully. He looked at the row of canned cat food on top of the file case.

"Yes, sir," said O'Connor uneasily, "but it's just temporary. We know who the dog's owner is, we just haven't been able to contact her yet—and we'll be finding a home for the cat just any day—but I know, that damn parrot, it's only, somebody's got to take care of it until the owner shows up, and we—"

The chief said explosively, "I don't care what the hell you do with it, but get it out of the lobby! I'm not going to have this place looking like a damned animal farm!"

"Yes, sir," said O'Connor. "I know what you mean, we'll see to it."

"Right now!" said the chief, and marched out, muttering about cats and parrots.

There wasn't, when they came to think it over, anywhere really convenient in the station to put Henry. The lab was too small, and Burt and Thomsen uttered outraged curses at the suggestion. The corridors were too narrow to accommodate the cage, and watch commander Gates firmly refused to have it in the Traffic mustering room. In the end O'Connor and Wallace trundled the cage up the stairs and heaved it up on top of the row of filing cases at the rear of the detective office. "Oh, my God," said Poor. Henry flapped and whistled, interested in his new surroundings. "Hello, dear, did you have a nice day? Give us a kiss, dear!"

"For God's sake," O'Connor asked Delia, "haven't you located this niece yet?"

"She won't be back until Monday," said Delia. "She's in Hawaii. It's just one of those things, Charles. The Humane Society won't have anything to do with him."

"And I can't say I blame them," said O'Connor bitterly. Delia went on with her list.

At five o'clock Gonzales and Forbes brought in a suspect to question, and they were still immured in an interrogation room when Mrs. Beal burst in on them. This time she had her husband with her, a big, good-natured-looking man. "The minute we got home and found she'd chewed through that rope, we knew where she was. I can't apologize enough! Making you all this trouble—but really you don't know whether to laugh or cry—" And suddenly Mrs. Beal was doing a little of both, getting out a handkerchief to wipe her eyes. "I tried to tell you before— she was my father's dog, and Dad died a couple of months ago— he was the chief of police in a little town called Paynes Creek away up north. She was at the police station with him every day, all the time—and I'll never know how she knew this is a police station, but—we were away all day, it was Harry's day off, we went down to San Diego to see his Aunt Clara in the convalescent home and take her a Christmas present—and as soon as I saw Rosie had chewed her rope—"

"I'll be damned," said Wallace, touched. "She's looking for him."

"Or she just figures," said Beal, "she belongs in a police station."

"It could be," said O'Connor, "there's a special smell about a police station—or policemen."

"A lot of the people we haul in here might agree with you," said Boswell.

"That's a funny one all right." Wallace bent to fondle Rosie's ears. "But it's not very safe for her getting out to run the streets, Mrs. Beal—there's quite a lot of traffic on Wilson—and if she persists in getting out of the yard—"

Beal opened his mouth, shut it, and then said meekly, "Well, you know—if it wasn't a bother—I could drop her off here on my way to work and pick her up every evening. She stays in at night all right."

"For the love of God!" said O'Connor, and then he started to laugh. "Well, why the hell not? You know, that's a very damn discriminating little dog, Mr. Beal—preferring the company of police officers. I will be damned." Rosie jumped into his lap and he fondled her crooked ears. "I don't think the chief would mind a dog—it's cats and parrots he's prejudiced about."

Varallo spent the day, belatedly, cutting back his roses. The storm had uprooted half a dozen of them; they were probably a total loss, and of course a couple of them had been prize specimens.

"It's a shame about Peace and Charlotte Armstrong," said Laura. "Two of my favorites."

"Well, they're both standard classics, I can replace them without any hunt. But it's a damned nuisance." He hadn't had a chance to do anything in the yard since the storm, and there was a lot of blown-in debris to clear up. It took him most of the day. And he wouldn't be able to get to a nursery to buy replacements until next week.

It was Harvey's night off. Rhys and Hunter were surprised to find Henry sharing the office, and after they'd sat around for an hour listening to his incessant chatter and fluttering and screeches, Rhys said desperately, "This is too much, Dick. Don't birds ever sleep?"

Hunter said dubiously, "I seem to remember—my aunt had a canary once—you're supposed to cover them up at night. It sends them to sleep. When we were at the Brent house that night, there was a blanket over the cage."

"Well, for God's sake let's find something," said Rhys. He went hunting, and the only thing he could locate was an old tarpaulin in the maintenance crew's closet in the basement. It wasn't big enough to cover the whole cage, but they draped it across the top and it seemed to serve as a hint to Henry. He stopped chattering and apparently went to sleep. "I should think somebody would have contacted the niece by now," said Rhys.

The weekend coming up again, business might be picking up. They had a call to a heist at ten o'clock, a drugstore down on South Brand, and the pharmacist was shaken up but keeping his head. He'd been the only one there; he told them he'd kept the place open half an hour later than usual as a favor to an old customer in a hurry for a prescription. The manager had left at the usual time. He gave a general description of the heister, who had, of course, taken all the usual pills as well as what was in the register. "But there wasn't much in it, of course. Mr. Bosley had taken all the day's receipts for the night deposit at the bank, there was just enough to start making change in the morning." The heister had been about twenty-five, medium-sized, a light-colored Negro with a mustache, and the pharmacist thought he'd recognize a picture. He'd come in tomorrow to make a statement and look at mug shots. They went back to the office, and Hunter did the initial report.

At eleven-forty they were called out to a homicide. It wasn't anything mysterious or interesting, just a simple crudity, a brawl in a bar on San Fernando Road, and one man pulling a knife. The dead man was Carlos Camacho, the knifer Louis Delgado. The bartender said they were both regulars, in several nights a week, and had never caused any trouble before, but tonight they'd got into an argument over something. It turned out to have been an argument over rival football teams, and Delgado had lost his temper. Rhys booked him into jail; this would just make more paperwork for the day watch. Hunter wrote the report. Henry was still mercifully asleep under his tarpaulin, and they didn't get another call all night. Tomorrow night might be different.

At the end of the shift on Saturday, Delia felt as tired as she'd ever felt in her life. She had started out on the legwork on that list this morning, and of course it was a job for one detective; if a couple of them tried to work it and one of them came across the big fat woman, there'd be no way to contact the others and call them off. There were eighty-seven names on the list, and the addresses were mostly in Glendale, a few in Burbank and Eagle Rock. But on Saturday the traffic was murder, and of course she hadn't found everybody home. She just wanted to look at all these women, and as an excuse was representing herself as inquiring for a witness to the incident at Buffums'. What with all the driving and a break for lunch, she had visited twenty-eight addresses and seen only eighteen of the women. Of course, Christmas coming up and the women out shopping—she would stand a better chance of catching them home in the evening and debated about having dinner somewhere and going back to cover the ones she'd missed, but her mind and body rebelled. After all, it was just a job, supposedly an eight-hour job. But she did stop at a restaurant on the way home, as a variation from the TV dinners, and as she sat over her preliminary drink, she suddenly thought that nobody had called the phone company to tell them about Ellen Lambert; they'd be wondering where she was. When she got home to the big gloomy house and had switched on lights and heat, she did that, and the supervisor she talked to was shocked. "Of course I knew her, a nice person, she'd worked this shift for about a year. We'd wondered about her, naturally, she was always punctual, and I'd been trying to call her—I was afraid there'd been an accident, because she was just fine on Wednesday night, so I didn't think she was down with flu or anything— Oh, I'm sorry to hear about this—very sorry. Of course I'll inform our personnel department, and thank you for letting us know."

Delia ran a boiling hot bath and spent some time relaxing in it. Now tomorrow morning she had the Myricks coming in; he had called Varallo this morning. There wasn't anything else to do about Lila Finch, or Nadine Parker. The burglars—there wasn't anywhere to go on that either. The job, she thought, could be a drag sometimes. Discouraging.

All three of them were on night watch on Saturday. When they came in, Henry was bouncing and chattering in his cage, and Harvey said, "They are sort of interesting at that—it's funny how they can talk."

"But this one doesn't know enough to shut up," said Hunter. "Thank God I remembered about covering him up." They found the tarpaulin folded on top of the filing case and covered the cage again and Henry went to sleep, or at least stopped talking.

Rhys went to look at the cat in O'Connor's office, and when he came back he said, "I think she's getting ready to produce those kittens. She's got the newspaper all torn up, and there's a look in her eye—"

Communications sent up their first call at nine-forty, a heist at a supermart on Glendale Avenue. Rhys said, "You two take it. I think I ought to stay with Mama cat, in case anything goes wrong. I've had a little experience at this sort of thing after all."

Harvey jeered, "Cat having kittens, what could go wrong?" Rhys said you never knew.

The heist kept Hunter and Harvey busy for quite a while; there'd been two heisters and a number of witnesses. About a dozen customers had still been in the store, and it had been a very slick pro job. One of them had herded the customers, three clerks, and the manager under one gun while the other had cleaned out all the registers. They had backed out the front door with the take and nobody had seen a car. But they got some unexpected help from the manager, who turned out to be a gun buff. "I couldn't say anything about the other gun," he told them, "the other guy was too far off, but the gun the first fellow had was a Colt Police Positive .38, just like you guys all carry. Sure I'm sure, guns I know." They got some descriptions, a better one of the man who'd guarded the witnesses. The consensus was that he was about forty, a white man with dark hair and a face described as tough. They had both worn dark slacks and windbreakers. The manager said savagely, "And they got a hell of a take—the whole Saturday's business, my God, we close at ten and half an hour later I'd have been bagging all the cash for the night deposit."

What with talking to all the witnesses, it was nearly eleven o'clock when Hunter and Harvey got back to the office, and Rhys met them with a broad grin. "Well, the new family's here, and very nice. I had to help her a little with the first one, but after that she did just fine." They went to look, and there were four of them. Rhys had lined the carton with fresh newspaper, and the cat, looking smug and dreamy, was lying on one side with the new arrivals lined up at the milk bar. Two of them were black, one gray tabby, and the fourth was white with indeterminate dark smudges. Harvey said, "My God, they're so little—"

"They're just fine," said Rhys. "They'll grow. Right now she won't want anybody handling them, we'll see if they're boys or girls later. Now we just find some nice homes for all of them, but they can't leave Mama for six weeks or so." He began to laugh. "My God, unless we find somebody to take Mama right away and look after the kittens until they can leave home, Charles is going to have a lively office in awhile. When they get their eyes open and start climbing out of that carton and running around, he'll need a nursery gate on his office door. I wonder if there's still a drugstore open anywhere."

"Why?" asked Harvey.

"I'd like to leave a cigar on his desk," said Rhys.

Sunday morning as the day watch came on, they all had to look at the kittens. The cat didn't seem to mind, if they didn't come too close or try to pick them up. She seemed to be spending most of the time washing them. Last night, Rhys hadn't found a drugstore open, but this morning Varallo went out and got a cigar to leave on O'Connor's desk.

On Saturday night, of course, there'd been two more burglaries, and Katz and Poor were both out.

Delia talked to the Myricks when they came in at ten o'clock. Fortunately her desk was at the front of the room and Henry's chatter wasn't too distracting.

"You can see, from our point of view there's just no way to investigate it any further. We didn't pick up any fingerprints in the house except ones which would naturally be there."

"But where is she?" asked Carla Myrick. "Even if she's dead, she'd have been found! I know you said—just the way Bob thought—she could have been attacked by somebody trying to break in, but why would anyone like that take her away? I don't understand what could have happened—"

Delia wasn't about to tell the Myricks what they had deduced about the Wash—and the ocean, and the fish. It was all speculation. She said, "We just don't know, Mrs. Myrick."

"But you think she's dead?" said Myrick. His eyes were hard and intelligent. "You do think that, don't you?"

"It's a pretty strong presumption, Mr. Myrick. When she hasn't been seen or heard of in this long a time, and the blood—" Carla Myrick gave a little sob.

He said heavily, "And without a body, that leaves it all up in the air. It'll be a legal tangle to sort out, but I know generally what's got to be done—a conservatorship for the estate, well, as her broker I could take that on. I'll have to see my lawyer, get things started." He shook his head. "A death—it's bad enough, when it's unexpected—but a thing like this—I just hate to think what could have happened to Lila."

Carla said incoherently, "She always enjoyed life so—and she was a good woman, she liked people, Miss Riordan, she gave to all sorts of charities and she did so enjoy going out shopping, and her bridge parties, and the theater—to think it should all end like this—"

"You're shutting down any investigation? Yes, I suppose so, there's nothing more for the police to do," said Myrick. He stood up. "Well, we can only thank you for what you have done, Miss Riordan. It's been an anxious time for us, but I guess we have to assume Lila's dead and take it from there." They went out quietly, his arm around her shoulders.

It was nearly eleven o'clock. Delia went out again on the list of names. On Sunday she should find more of the women home, and the traffic wasn't so thick. By the end of the day, she had seen all the women she had missed yesterday, and a few more. She had seen fat women, thin women, old and young and middle-aged women, at a variety of addresses ranging from expensive apartments to houses and condominiums, but she hadn't seen any big fat woman with white hair, a double chin, and a hooked nose.

And the forecast was for more rain.

O'Connor was still at the station at five o'clock, but keeping out of his office in deference to the evident desire of Mama cat for privacy. When he got a call from that LAPD lieutenant, Daley, he got the desk to transfer it to Varallo's phone. Daley was sounding pleased and amused. "You remember my mentioning Tony Sardo to you?"

"Vividly," said O'Connor.

"Well, how would you like to join a little raid? We've pinpointed the supply drop."

"For God's sake, how?"

Daley laughed. "Never underestimate the power of a woman. Sardo's been married for twenty years to a platinum blond ex-hoofer named Magda, and she walked into the captain's office this afternoon and opened her mouth wide."

"Goddamn," said O'Connor. "Why?"

"Reasons," said Daley. "She's good and mad at him because he's planning to dump her legally for a cute little redheaded hostess at his fancy restaurant. She knows everything there is to know about his affairs, and she's not about to take even a hefty settlement when she can keep the whole kit and caboodle with him in the pen. She offered us the deal cool as bedamned, all she knows about Sardo and the dealers under him for immunity from prosecution as accessory."

"Now I will be damned," said O'Connor.

"We asked her if she wasn't worried about the Syndicate taking a little revenge, and she said Tony's on the skids with his bosses anyway, they'd be putting him out to pasture any day. They'd be annoyed at losing a batch of fairly high-up dealers, but there were always more to be had."

"And she told you where the drop is?"

"Yeah, it's in an eighth-floor office in one of your new high-rises on North Brand, rented under the name of the United Insurance Company. She says there's usually a meeting on Sunday nights to hand out the wholesale stashes to local dealers. It's your territory, and we thought we'd gate-crash the meeting. Like to join the party?"

"You're damn right. When and where?"

"We'll meet you at your station at seven," said Daley.

"I'll be waiting for you," said O'Connor, "with bells on!"

When the night watch came on on Sunday night, they didn't know anything about the raid. They sat around waiting for a call and listened to Henry's screeching and chattering until Rhys hunted around for the tarpaulin, which had gotten carried into O'Connor's office, and covered the cage. Henry subsided, and they listened to the calls on the police frequency for lack of anything else to do.

They were galvanized into action at a quarter past nine when the reports started to come in that there was a lot of gunfire going on somewhere up on North Brand. "What the hell?" said Hunter. "An office building, for God's sake—" A squad had been passing when it started and called in for backup.

"We'd better get up there," said Harvey urgently. They piled out in a hurry.

When they got to the scene, there were five squads with doors hanging open and the uniformed men were cussing a blue streak. The doors of the building were locked and they couldn't get in. "It's stopped now," said Bill Watkins, "about ten minutes ago—it was on one of the upper floors—Steiner got the emergency number off the door and went to call the building manager—"

They hung around waiting, and about five minutes later the front door of the building opened and a crowd of men came out. About a dozen of them were wearing handcuffs, and there were a dozen more riding herd on them. The night watch heard a familiar voice raised in some unprintable language, and surged forward.

"What the hell are all of you doing here?" demanded O'Connor. "Some son of a bitch winged me, by God—" He hadn't holstered the .357 magnum, but it was in his left hand.

Another man said, "You're bleeding like a stuck pig, apologies, O'Connor. You'd better get over to emergency, we'll take 'em in."

"They're your property anyway. Goddamn it, this is nearly a new suit—well, thanks very much for the entertainment."

"For God's sake, what's been going on here?" asked Rhys. O'Connor told them while they ferried him down to the emergency ward at the Memorial Hospital. He'd taken a slug from a .38 through his upper arm, but it wasn't anything serious. And the LAPD boys had shut down a wholesale dope-dealing gang for a while at least. There'd be replacements put in. That kind of thing went on forever.

Katharine called Varallo to tell him about it at eleven-thirty, and she sounded cross. "And if I know Charles, he'll want to go to the office as usual, and I've got an appointment to have a permanent at nine A.M. If he shows up, you chase him right back home, Vic. No, no, he'll be all right, but the doctor gave him some pain pills and said he might have a little temperature in the morning and he'd better stay in bed."

"Well, I'll do my best, but we both know Charles," said Varallo.

Patrolman Albert Morris had never seriously thought about bucking for rank; he liked riding a squad. The thought had crossed his mind that the detective work might be interesting, but there was a hell of a lot of paperwork to it, and he wasn't sure he had that kind of brain. After this Monday he thought just maybe he might.

He'd been cruising the beat since eight o'clock, and had handed out one ticket, but he didn't get a call until twelve-thirty. He'd been just about to call in a Code Seven and go and have lunch, and he swore, but he said into the mike, "Roger." The address was on Glendale Avenue, and when he got there, it was a smallish tan stucco building with a sign over the entrance, Underwood Institute for Exceptional Children. Morris thought to himself that there was a lot of double-talk used these days; they were now calling the morons exceptional. He went into a long empty hallway, and a woman came toward him from the far end of it, a tall, thin woman in a plain black dress.

"What's the trouble here, ma'am?"

She said severely, "Everything's all right now, we shouldn't have troubled you, Officer. Miss Keller just lost her head for a moment. You needn't stay, it's all right."

"Well, what happened, ma'am?"

"Just a little scuffle between two of the boys, but Lonnie had a knife—" She was looking angry. She said remotely, as if to herself, "I'll call Mrs. Alderson immediately, this is really becoming insupportable, we'll have to ask her to take him away, he's too much of a disruptive influence. But it's nothing to do with the police, Officer."

Morris said patiently, "Ma'am, I've got to make a report when I'm called, just tell me what's been going on here."

She said a little reluctantly, "This is a private school for exceptional children, as I'm sure you noticed. They are mostly retarded in various degrees, and none of them what could be termed mentally disturbed, but since the new term we've had one boy here, Bobby Alderson, who's been very difficult and disruptive. He bullies the other children, they're afraid of him, and he's really not capable of learning much—but I was surprised at the other boy, Lonnie Snyder, he's always been a good boy, never any trouble."

"That's the boy who had the knife?" asked Morris.

"Yes. Miss Keller took it away from him, of course, and Bobby only got a scratch, though from the yells you'd have thought he was murdered."

"I think I'd better see the knife, ma'am. Are you the head of the school?"

"Yes, I'm Mrs. Underwood. Well, if you must—" She took him down to a small office at the end of the hall, past a couple of bigger rooms. A woman and a boy were sitting there, the woman sniffing into a handkerchief.

"I'm sorry I panicked, Mrs. Underwood, but when I saw that knife— Mrs. Dietrich's bandaging Bobby's arm, it was just a scratch—"

There was a knife on the desk. It had a long, narrow blade and an imitation bone handle. Morris looked at it and at the boy. Anybody could see he was retarded. He looked by his size to be about sixteen, but he had a heavy, fat, foolish face with a slack, wet mouth, dull eyes, and a very bad case of acne making ugly scars. Morris looked at the knife again and something clicked in his mind, and all of a sudden he thought about that girl stabbed in the public library. If they let these kids roam around— He hadn't seen the autopsy report, but he thought, the library only about six blocks away—and he said to Mrs. Underwood, "I'd like to use a phone here. A private phone." She was still reluctant but took him into her office. He called the station and talked to Sergeant Varallo.

"I may be just woolgathering, Sergeant, but I think maybe you ought to have a look at this kid."

The law was very touchy about citizens' rights, especially ones like Lonnie Snyder. Varallo and Forbes went up to the school, got the name and address of Lonnie's mother, and called her. They took Lonnie in and sat him down under the eye of Mary Champion, with Guernsey sitting in. He was a little scared at new faces, but he was a polite, quiet boy, and somebody had taught him manners. When his mother arrived, she was more frightened than he was.

"Why have you got Lonnie here? Lonnie's a good boy, he never does anything wrong—"

"We're not saying he did, Mrs. Snyder," said Varallo. "But he had a knife. Do you know where he got it?" He showed it to her. She said, "Why, that looks like one of my kitchen knives, I hadn't missed it— Lonnie, did you take that out of the kitchen drawer?" He nodded once.

"Why?" asked Varallo. "Why did you want it, Lonnie?"

"Because I was scared," he said hoarsely. "Bobby, most of the kids at school are scared of Bobby, he hits us—I thought, he hit me again, I stick that into him."

"Did you ever stick it into anyone else, Lonnie? How long have you had it?"

He looked confused at two questions at once. He said, "I dunno. I never stuck it in Bobby before."

"Were you ever in the library, Lonnie?" He nodded jerkily. Varallo looked at Mrs. Snyder. "I don't suppose you let him go around alone—"

"Of course not, he's always with me when he's not in school— What's this all about?"

"Were you at the public library a week ago Saturday? In the afternoon? Was Lonnie with you?"

"Why, yes, I was— I wasn't there long—he just sat in a chair and waited for me. He's always been a good, quiet boy, a terrible grief to my husband and me he's the way he is—our only one —but he's a quiet, good boy."

"Do you remember seeing a girl at the library?" Varallo asked Lonnie. "A pretty, dark-haired girl?"

He shuffled his feet awkwardly, and now his dull eyes were full of dumb resentment. Suddenly he said in his hoarse voice, "She looked at me funny. I was just waiting in the chair like Mama said, I wasn't doing nothing, but she looked funny at me —girls always look funny at me, I don't like girls—and—and—I been thinkin' about stickin' the knife into Bobby—how it'd feel —and I had it in my pocket—and I just stuck it into that girl, because she looked at me funny. But she didn't yell or try to run away or nothing, I guess I just didn't stick it in far enough—"

Mrs. Snyder let out a little scream, and Varallo said sadly to Forbes, "So now we know."

CHAPTER 10

Of course, Lonnie wouldn't come to trial. There would be a psychiatric evaluation and a judicial hearing, and he'd probably end up in Atascadero. He'd never, according to what they'd heard, exhibited any violence before, but now that he had, there could be a next time. And now somebody would have to tell the Parkers why they'd lost their nice, ambitious, bright daughter. For the moment, Lonnie landed in Juvenile Hall, and Mary got Mrs. Snyder calmed down sufficiently to go home and call her husband. There'd be a lot of paperwork on this, and conferences at the D.A.'s office.

Delia came in at five o'clock, heard about it, and said tiredly, "Oh, God. One like that. Just at random, and that nice, promising girl—somebody else can talk to the Parkers. I'm beat, and I'm going home early." But before she left she called the Foley house in Eugene, Oregon. She got the house sitter again.

"Oh, they're staying on a couple of extra days, I had a wire just today, they say they'll be home on Thursday now." Delia sat back in her desk chair and regarded Henry in the cage across the office. She had been out all day on that damned list of the check writers, but there were the necessary things to do and nobody else seemed to be disposed to do them. She had got Burt to put the lettuce and fruit into the refrigerator at the lab, though he'd complained about it. She went wearily downstairs, brought up another couple of oranges and the rest of the lettuce, and refilled one feeding dish with sunflower seeds. "You're a very pretty girl, dear," said Henry ingratiatingly. "Let's all have a little drink! Scratch Henry's head! Yo-ho and a bottle of rum!"

On her way home she couldn't help thinking about Lonnie and Nadine Parker, and it was an exercise in futility. These

things happened, and you couldn't get emotionally involved.
But thank God she was off tomorrow.

At noon on Tuesday Thomsen called the detective office.
Varallo and Forbes were just on the point of leaving to have
lunch. "We just got the kickback on those prints. From the
wrench in Ralston's apartment. The Feds had them."

"So we take the shortcut," said Varallo. "Good. He's got a
pedigree?"

"No," said Thomsen. "He did a hitch in the Army about ten
years ago. His name is Lloyd Fosdick, and the last home address
they had for him was Peoria, Illinois. I'll send up a teletype."

"Maybe not a shortcut," said Varallo. He and Forbes went out
to lunch at the coffee shop down the block, and when they got
back, the teletype was on his desk.

Forbes said, "There could be a relative who knows where he
is now." Varallo agreed, got Information, got the phone number, and called Peoria. After three rings a woman answered,
and it was Fosdick's mother. Varallo told her he was an old army
buddy of Lloyd's trying to locate him, and could she tell him
where he was? "Why, he's out in California now," she said, and
parted readily with an address in Burbank. Varallo put the
phone down and said, "Let's go see if he's home." He wasn't
there—it was a small, cheap apartment on the outskirts of town
—but the owner lived on the premises and could tell them
where he worked, at a garage on Magnolia Boulevard.

Fosdick was a nondescript-looking man about thirty-five; they
found him working on the transmission of an old Buick. Varallo
showed him the badge. "We'd like to ask you a few questions,
Fosdick."

"What about?"

"We'll talk at the station," said Forbes.

Fosdick said, "The boss won't appreciate my walking off the
job. Cops!"

"That's too bad," said Varallo. He didn't make any further
objections to going with them. At the station they took him into
an interrogation room, and Varallo said, "About Calvin Ralston,
Fosdick," and sudden comprehension and alarm showed in Fos-

dick's expression. He sat rigidly in the straight chair and said, "Who?"

"You were in his apartment with him one night last week—Tuesday night, a week ago today." They'd had the autopsy report now, and that was the estimated time of death.

"I don't know any Calvin Ralston."

Forbes said gently, "We found your prints there, Fosdick."

For a minute he didn't say anything, and then he came out with a few obscenities. "For Christ's sake, you mean he had the guts to call the cops in on it? Listen, I never pulled anything like that before, damn it, but the guy just riled me—"

"How?" asked Varallo.

Fosdick said disgustedly, "And you can call me a goddamned fool. I've been around, I'm no hayseed from the sticks, but I never suspected that guy was a fag! He riled me plenty."

"Where'd you meet him?" asked Forbes.

"Well, I guess he told you, I ran into him at a bar on Alameda. I'd just stopped in for a drink before dinner, and he was on the next stool, and we got to talking. It never entered my head he was a fag, he seemed like a straight-enough guy—and I'm kind of a Second World War buff and he said he was too, and he had some interesting photographs, would I like to see them, and he asked me to his pad—and then, by God, when I got there he propositions me, and I was riled as hell, him thinking he could pay me to be his little pal—me! You'd think I was just off the farm, I didn't spot him before—" He snorted.

"So you banged him on the head with that wrench?" said Varallo.

Fosdick, still disgusted with himself, said shortly, "Well, you know that. I never thought he'd do anything about it, one that kind— Yeah, I was so riled at him, I did it without thinking, I had the damn wrench in my back pocket, I'd just come off work—and I cut out of there in a hurry and it wasn't till I got home I remembered I'd left the wrench there— So he decided to blow the whistle on me, huh? You're going to charge me with assault or something?"

"Something," said Varallo. "You killed him, Fosdick. He's dead."

Fosdick sat up and let out an incredulous expletive. "You're not serious? Just that bang on the head? Well, I'll be good and goddamned!"

When Delia came back on the job on Wednesday morning, she heard about that from O'Connor, who'd been induced to stay home a couple of days nursing his bullet wound but had come in this morning and was sitting at Varallo's desk with Rosie at his feet. "One cleaned up anyway. And it'll get called involuntary manslaughter, he'll get a one-to-three and be out in ten months. No big deal, and Ralston's no loss. When the hell are you going to do anything about that damned bird?"

"Hopefully tomorrow," said Delia. She had got a *Times* downstairs and proceeded to change the papers in Henry's cage and refill his feeding dishes. Henry whistled at her and swung back and forth on his swing. "Thank you, dear! You're a very pretty girl! Did you have a nice day? Scratch Henry's head!"

A couple of people had picked out some mug shots, and Varallo and Forbes were out hunting for those men. O'Connor was alone in the office; probably Katz and Poor had a new burglary to cope with. Delia went out again to get on with her list of check writers. The only thing she knew for certain was that the big fat woman had to be on the list, and probably she'd be the very last one.

But that afternoon about three o'clock she found her. Her name was Stephanie Coatesworth and she lived in an unpretentious single house on Idlewood Road. She answered the door herself, and Delia took one look at her and said, "I'd like to ask you a few questions, Mrs. Coatesworth." She brought out the badge. Mrs. Coatesworth was at least five-ten, a big-boned woman, and fat, and she had white hair in tight little curls and a high-bridged nose with a little hook in it. She looked at the badge. "Police," she said. "What kind of questions?" She let Delia into an orderly and comfortable living room. "Sit down and tell me what it's about." She was quite friendly and natural.

"It's about the woman you pushed down the escalator at Buffums' last Thursday, Mrs. Coatesworth." She hadn't sat down, but Mrs. Coatesworth did, subsiding heavily onto the couch. She stared at Delia.

"How'd you know about that?" she asked weakly.

"We had your description."

"Oh, dear, oh, dear, what an upset—police finding out, coming—I suppose she'll sue me, and Fred'll be furious, and it's my own fault—I was sorry the second I'd done it, I've always had a quick temper— I know I shouldn't have hit her, and I'm sorry—"

"Why did you hit her, Mrs. Coatesworth?"

She got a handkerchief out of her pocket and blew her nose, wiped her eyes. "My awful temper," she said. "I was so tired that day, it had been an awful day, the kind when everything goes wrong, you know? I'd put in a load of laundry and there was something wrong with the dryer, and try to get a repair man—especially this time of year—and then the toaster wouldn't work, we've needed a new one for a while, and the price they are now—and I still had all that shopping to do. I don't know anything more tiring than Christmas shopping, some people are easy but some you just don't know what to get, and about the worst is Fred's sister Marge, she's so fussy. It was on account of that, you see. I'd got the grandchildren all taken care of, and my sister and aunt, but I hadn't got anything for Marge yet, and I was looking at housecoats and I found one I thought would do—it was more than I meant to spend but most things are—it was the only one like it in her size—but I wasn't quite sure, I'd just hung it over the rack—and that woman was there, she saw me do it and she must have known I was coming back to get it as soon as I made up my mind. I just went across the aisle to look at nightgowns, but I decided on the housecoat instead, and when I went back that woman had just bought it, the only possible one in Marge's size, and I was furious—now I'd have to go looking for something else all over again, and I was so tired—and I followed her over to the escalator, I told her just what I thought of her, snatching it out from under me when she could see I wanted to buy it. Oh, dear, I was mad—but she just looked at me as if she didn't know what I was talking about, and my temper got the better of me and I hit her—I just reached out and hit her, and walked away."

"She fell down the escalator, you know," said Delia.

"No, I didn't know," said Mrs. Coatesworth. "I didn't mean to do her any real harm, I was just mad. I'm sorry now, I was sorry the minute I'd done it."

"She's dead, Mrs. Coatesworth. She fell down and fractured her skull on the escalator."

Mrs. Coatesworth stared at her in consternation. "Oh, my goodness," she said feebly, "I can't believe—I never thought—" And of course, this would be another charge of involuntary manslaughter.

"I'll have to ask you to come downtown with me," said Delia.

She said faintly, "You mean—to jail? You're going to arrest me? Oh, my goodness, what will Fred say—I can't believe this is happening—can I call my husband? I've got to call Fred—and the Andersons are coming for dinner—and I haven't got those packages wrapped for mailing yet—oh, dear, Fred's always said my temper would get me in trouble some day—but I just can't believe I *killed* somebody—"

Delia let her call her husband and drove her downtown to the jail. She'd just got into the office when the husband arrived, a fat man very shocked and shaken, and had to be told all about it. Like a lot of people, he didn't know the first thing about the law, and she explained about bail, about bail bondsmen, and told him he could see his wife anytime. It was after five by then, and she could write the report tomorrow. Varallo was the only one in and had sat in on the talk with the husband.

"Little lesson in how not to shop," he said. "That was a queer one."

"And a lot of legwork for a minor matter," said Delia. "But we had to look, and find her." She fed Henry and went wearily home.

Hunter and Harvey came on and discovered that Henry's tarpaulin was missing. Henry was in his usual form, and they turned the office upside down hunting for it before Hunter found it had slid down behind the file cases. They fished it out, draped it over the cage, and Henry subsided. They had a look at the kittens. At nine-forty a call came in to a heist and they went out on it. It was a pharmacy on Broadway. The uniformed man was Whalen, and he said, "You got him. The manager's an expro heavyweight, he was in the stock room when the guy pulled the gun on the pharmacist, and he jumped him from behind."

At the pharmacy counter a big, heavy-shouldered man and a smaller one were standing over a weird-looking creature. The first man said, "Here's his gun," and handed Harvey a Colt automatic. "These damn creeps. Take him away. And don't tell me, I know, he'll get about six months in the joint and be out again."

The heister was male, and his head was shaved naked except for one long strand of blond hair in a braid halfway down his back. He wore a single gold earring and a gold stud in one nostril. He had on an orange silk shirt and skintight black pants and a bright red pea coat. He looked about twenty-five. They took him out to the car, and Harvey said, "So let's have your name."

"Driscoll," he said sullenly. "Kevin Driscoll." Hunter got in the backseat with him, and they started downtown to book him in. On the way he said resentfully, "I just had to get hold of some bread, you got to eat and pay the rent and all. I've been trying to get a job, but nobody'll hire me at any damn thing, they look at me like I'm something from Mars, they say go away and fix myself up decent—that's what that dame at the employment agency said—"

"So why don't you?" asked Hunter. "You can't expect anybody to hire you when you're got up like a freak show."

"Man," said Driscoll with dignity, "I got a right to my own life-style, I'm a free spirit, I got the right not to conform to all the stupid middle-class values—you damn cops just like the rest of them, only worse, never give anybody an even break if they're different from everybody else—" He was still talking about being a free spirit when they booked him in. He had three dollars and half a dozen marijuana cigarettes on him.

Delia got in a little late on Thursday morning. Varallo and Gonzales were talking to a citizen, Katz typing a report, and Poor on the phone. "Would you recognize a photograph of the man who held you up?" Varallo was asking.

The citizen, a bald, middle-aged man, said abstractedly, "I guess so, he wasn't three feet from me, I was behind the counter—" But he seemed more interested in Henry than everyday questions; he stared at the cage across the room. "Is it a mascot, like?" he asked suddenly. "I mean, it's a funny place to find a parrot."

O'Connor, at Boswell's desk, said forcefully, "We couldn't agree with you more."

And a bent little old lady came hesitantly into the office, looking around doubtfully, and Delia went over to her. "Can we do something for you?" she asked kindly.

"I don't know," said the woman. "Mr. Jewett said to see the police. Miss Gilligan said she thought there was something wrong, and Mr. Jewett at the bank said I should tell the police."

"Well, sit down and tell me what it's about. May I have your name?"

She was a very little old lady, with a round, wrinkled face and bright brown eyes and a cloud of white hair. She sat in the chair beside Delia's desk and said, "Well, they seemed like nice young men. So well dressed. I'd never seen them at the bank, but they said they were in the accounting department. I'm Mrs. Jarvis, Mrs. Emily Jarvis. They came to see me about two weeks ago, a Mr. Johnson and a Mr. Boone. They said the bank suspected one of the tellers was stealing money and asked if I'd help them prove it. They wanted me to draw out most of my money in cash, and then they'd mark the bills and put it back in my account or something, I'm not quite clear just how it would help them prove the teller was stealing, but they said it would. And they even drove me down to the bank. I usually take the bus, unless Miss Gilligan happens to be going downtown and takes me in her car, she's my next-door neighbor. And so I did, and gave them the money—"

"How much?" asked Delia.

"Oh, it was nearly two thousand dollars. You see, I don't spend all that comes in, I really don't need much these days, I own the house, and I've got my husband's railroad pension and that nice stock my father left me. There'd have been more than that, but I'd just paid the first installment on the taxes. And they said the money would be paid back into my account right away, but it hasn't been, and yesterday I asked Mr. Jewett about it, and he said I'd been swindled and I'd better go to the police. He was annoyed about it, he said something about it being an old game." She looked anxiously at Delia. And Delia thought, my God, one of the oldest con games going, and still taking in the innocent old ladies. And of course polite Mr. Johnson and Mr. Boone had faded into the woodwork.

"Can you describe the men?" she asked.

Of course she couldn't. "Then it was a swindle, and I won't get my money back? Oh, dear."

"I'm afraid not, Mrs. Jarvis."

"Oh, dear. Miss Gilligan thought so, and Mr. Jewett said—" There wasn't anything to do about this one either. Delia asked if she could get home all right. "Oh, yes, my dear, I've always been a good walker, and it's only four blocks up to Brand where I get the bus."

Delia called the bank and talked to Jewett, who was the assistant manager. He said, "So she did go to see you, I was going to call in on it sometime today. These damn bunco artists, I thought everybody'd heard of that old game, and such a nice little old lady too—it's a damn shame." Delia said that was the kind they went for. She sat back in her chair and lit a cigarette, and Katz came in. Varallo, Forbes, and Gonzales had gone out hunting more heisters. Katz sat down at his desk and scowled at Henry, who said in a lascivious tone, "You're a very pretty girl, dear! I like a little sugar in my tea!" "Have you had any inspiration on the burglars?" asked Katz.

"Well, I picked up one thing they have in common, Joe—the victims. None of them drives or has a car."

"Oh, I spotted that. The reason it was in the reports. I went around on it some. That's natural, most of them did drive, but they'd either got so they couldn't pass the test anymore, vision or something, or couldn't afford to keep up a car now. I'd thought about cab companies, you know, if they took cabs to the market or shopping, but that's out too, some of them have relatives somewhere around and the rest have friends here and there who drive them places, or they take the bus. They can't afford cabs."

"Oh," said Delia.

"Let's all have a little drink!" suggested Henry loudly.

Katz said sardonically, "That's a good idea but not very practical in a puritanical police station."

After the legwork of the last few days, this day dragged. Rosie got up in Katz's lap. Delia went to look at the kittens. The clock got around to noon, and she went out to lunch with Mary Champion. She had just got back at one-thirty when her phone rang. A high, thin voice announced itself as Linda Foley.

"I was just devastated to hear about Aunt Lydia, we got home an hour ago and Wilma told me you had called. Of course, we all knew about her heart, that she could go any time, but it was a shock."

"Oh, Mrs. Foley, I'm so glad you've called. Are you planning to come down here?"

"Yes, of course—we'll want to arrange the funeral, she owned a plot in Forest Lawn—and there'll be the house to clear out. I know she'd left everything to me, there'll be probate before we can put the house up for sale—"

"And there's Henry," said Delia. "The parrot. We've been taking care of it—him—but—"

Linda Foley said sharply, "That thing! Oh, I don't want that. Uncle Bernie and Aunt Lydia doted on it, I never could understand it. I don't care what happens to the parrot, you give it away or better yet send it to the Humane Society and let them put it out of its misery. I suppose the police have the keys to the house? Well, we'll be down sometime tomorrow."

Delia put the phone down and looked at Henry, who was eating a piece of orange greedily and didn't look particularly miserable. She said, "The niece doesn't want the parrot."

"Well, of all the ungrateful people," said Katz, "after we've gone to all the trouble of looking after the damn thing, putting up with it all this while—so what the hell do we do with it now?"

O'Connor looked up from reading a report. "Personally I don't give a damn what you do with it so long as you get it out of the office."

Delia sighed. She went over and reached into the cage to scratch Henry's head. They had all complained about it, but she liked Henry; he was cheerful and amusing. She sat and smoked another cigarette, and then she went downstairs to the lab. Burt and Thomsen were both busy at the workbench.

"Would you do me a little favor, Rex?" asked Delia. "At the end of shift, could you load that cage onto a van and bring it over to my house?"

"What," said Burt, "are you going to adopt that fool bird?"

"Well," said Delia, "nobody seems to want him. He's got no family at all." Just like me, she thought.

Thomsen laughed. "I hope you know what you're getting into. Sure, we can do that for you."

The night watch didn't get a call until ten-forty, and when Rhys and Harvey got there, it was a modest single house on Pioneer Drive. The squad was in front, and Whalen was on the porch. "Oh-oh," said Rhys. "Want to bet?"

It was the pair of knowledgeable burglars again. The victim this time was Miss Shirley Lane. She was a little wiry, gray-haired woman, and quite composed and in control. She told them the same story they'd heard before, the announcement of police at the door, prowler in the backyard, the need to use the phone, the stocking masks, the knife. They'd taken all the cash out of her handbag, nothing else. "But," she added briskly, "I can tell you who one of them was."

Incredulously Rhys asked, "How? If they had on masks—"

She nodded. "Nylon stockings pulled down, a most uncanny effect. But I recognized his voice, you see."

"What do you mean?" asked Harvey.

"My dear young man, I taught voice and drama for forty years, I have perfect pitch and a perfect ear. All the while they were here and the one with the knife was talking—to me and the other one—I was thinking, Now where have I heard that voice before? And then it came to me. It was the young man who came from Republican headquarters to drive me to the polls on election day in November."

"My God in heaven," said Rhys. "Are you sure?"

"Absolutely," she said. "It's quite a distinctive individual voice, a light baritone with just a suggestion of a lisp. Of course I don't know his name, but I expect you could find that out."

"By God, by God," said Katz to Delia on Friday morning, "could this be? Are we going to get a break at last?"

"Of all the queer things," said Delia, rereading Rhys's report.

"They do that," said Katz. "Both parties, they send around notices to the voters, if they need a ride to the polls, somebody will drive them. By God—let's get on the phone! Gimme half of those reports, you call the other half!"

Three quarters of an hour later, they put their phones down nearly simultaneously and looked at each other. "Jackpot!" said Katz gleefully. "The link, by God—and a very funny one it is." Every single one of those victims had called into Republican headquarters and asked for a ride to the polls.

"But it would be just a temporary office, Joe—it was a store on South Brand, I remember the sign. They only maintain a local office during the campaign. Volunteers distributing literature and so on."

"I know, I know, but there'll be a permanent party headquarters somewhere around—" He was leafing through the yellow pages. "There you are, downtown L.A. And they'll know which local Republicans were manning the campaign fronts." He seized the phone and dialed. He got a brisk, efficient-sounding woman who told him they had only opened local offices during the campaign—oh, he wanted to know who had been the volunteer workers in the Glendale office, well, she didn't have that information, but if he'd wait a moment, she could tell him who had been responsible for managing it. She came back on the line three minutes later and said, "It was Mr. John Colfax, he's one of our most dedicated political workers. Oh, it's Colfax and Hadley," and she gave him an address on North Brand.

"Come on!" said Katz to Delia. "Don't tell me we're closing in!"

It was a fourth-floor office in one of the newer buildings, and Colfax and Hadley were attorneys-at-law. Katz showed the badge to a nice-looking, dark-haired secretary in the outer office. "We'd like to see Mr. Colfax, please. No, sorry, we haven't got an appointment, but it's urgent." She went into one of the two inner offices and came back with a tall affable-looking middle-aged man.

He looked at the badge and asked, "What can I do for the police?"

"You headed up the local Republican office here during the

campaign," said Katz. "I suppose it was all staffed with volunteers—"

"Yes, that's right, mailing out campaign literature, answering phone inquiries, and so forth. Why?"

"And you sent out notices to all the registered voters, whoever needed to be driven to their balloting places to call in and ask?"

"Yes, we always do that. It's chiefly elderly people who otherwise would have no way to get out and vote."

"Who actually did the driving, do you remember? Were there many people who called in and asked for rides?"

Colfax adjusted his glasses. "Really, what all this is about—I don't know the exact figure, Mrs. Magnusson made up the list of names as the people called in, I suppose there might have been as many as forty or fifty. Well, there were five or six people who volunteered their time and cars to do that, all election day. As they came into the office, Mrs. Magnusson or one of the other women would have given them a list of, say, eight or ten names, from the list of people who called in. Really—" He was looking very curious.

"Most of the volunteers were women? I suppose they're the ones with more free time, the ones who don't work. Was there a man in on that, doing the driving of people to vote?"

"Why, my son was one of them—all the rest were women, that's right. My son Richard. I've always considered it very important for a good citizen to be politically active—I'm afraid he doesn't take much interest yet, but he's only in his first year of college. I encouraged him to skip his classes that day and help us out— What in the world is this all about?" asked Colfax plaintively.

He was a very good-looking, dark young fellow with a fresh complexion and a wide mobile mouth, with the suggestion of a dimple in one cheek. Katz towed him in on the stroke of noon and sat him down beside Delia's desk. "What the hell is this all about?" he asked. "You saying questions, getting me out of class—" But he knew. His eyes were watchful, and he eyed O'Connor and the bulge of the .357 magnum warily.

Katz said coldly, "We needn't waste time, Colfax. It's been

you and one of your pals who've been pulling all these burglaries of the old people. You got hold of that list—the people who called in asking for rides to the polls—when the campaign front closed down, and that was how you knew all the names. We've got a witness who recognized you now."

"Recognized me? How the hell could—" He stopped abruptly.

"Could she do that, when you were wearing a stocking mask? Well, she did, and I think she'll be a good witness," said Katz.

He didn't say anything for a minute, and then he flung himself back in the chair and uttered an excited, reckless laugh. "Oh, my God, my father'll have a stroke. His one ewe lamb. And I don't know how the hell anybody ever found out. It just started out as a kind of game—but God, I'm always short of money and so is Johnny. Oh, I'll tell you—Johnny Gallagher—I'm not taking the rap alone, no way. Yeah, I got roped into helping out the good little Republicans on election day, and I came across that list when they were clearing up the place after the polls closed. I thought it was a sort of bright idea, and so did Johnny—we even had a uniform to make it look more kosher—Johnny's dad's old army uniform. And it worked like a charm. We tried to play it cautious, I said no jewelry because it might get identified, skip most stuff except cash. Johnny did take a watch, one place, a nice new one to give his girl for Christmas. And it was working just like a charm— How the hell did the cops ever find out about it?"

O'Connor gave him his shark's grin. "Never underestimate the power of a woman," he said. "Some of these docile, doddering old folks are the hell of a lot smarter than you young punks."

"And damn it to hell," said Katz after he'd booked him at the jail and was ready to go and locate the other one, "you know the D.A. is going to balk at a charge of involuntary manslaughter on Lydia Brent—and it's a first count for both of them. They'll get a one-to-three and be out in ten months."

"At least you've got them," said O'Connor.

Delia felt a little foolish about it, but in the evenings, on her day off, and as she passed the cage coming and going, she found herself talking to Henry. She'd got a book about parrots at the library.

"My name's Delia, can you say Delia? Delia, Henry." He cocked his bright head at her and winked his beady eyes, and he said a good many other things. She thought that when the house got sold and she found a nice little apartment, she'd have to do something about a different cage. That enormous thing was taking up most of the dining room table.

They had the usual number of heists, and another suicide, to make more paperwork. And on the day of Christmas Eve, Delia was at her desk talking to Varallo, O'Connor, and Forbes about a new attempted rape, when the Myricks came into the office. They were both looking half indignant and half amused. They sat down and looked at the men, at Delia, and Myrick said, "We thought you'd better know. First of all I'll tell you that I went up to check on the house yesterday, and that gardener was there. He always comes on Wednesdays. I talked a little to him, and I told him how we were afraid something had happened to Lila, and I mentioned the blood in the garage, and he said right off, oh, that was him. He had a little accident, he said, it was the day before Thanksgiving, he'd broken a bottle of liquid fertilizer and given himself a bad cut, had quite a time stopping the bleeding."

"Oh," said Varallo blankly.

Carla Myrick uttered a half hysterical laugh. "And Bob was just telling me about that when the mail came—" She opened her bag, took out an envelope, and thrust it at Delia. "Go ahead, read it—you deserve to read it! My God, she put down the wrong zip code, transposed two numbers, and the post office— the service gets worse and worse—it's been all over the place by the postmarks—Fresno and Modesto and Visalia—of course, she expected it'd be waiting for us when we got home the Monday after Thanksgiving! My God, I don't like it, but after what we've been thinking—go ahead and read it!"

Varallo came to read it over Delia's shoulder, O'Connor beside him. It was on good-quality note paper, in Lila Finch's square, plain writing, and it was dated the day after Thanksgiving.

"My dears, you're going to call me a very naughty old lady, but I hope you'll try to understand. I'm getting married again, and please don't think I'm being foolish, because it's going to be all right, it's going to be wonderful. I can hear Bob swearing about fortune hunters and silly old women, but children, he's got more money than I have! His name is George Elmore and we met in Dr. Spaulding's office when I went in for my flu shot, wasn't it queer?—just as if it were meant. We hit it off right away, he reminds me a little of Lou—and he's been lonely too, he lost his wife five years ago. They hadn't any family either. He's just my age. We've been out together a good deal, and we enjoy all the same things and are such good companions. We decided last week to get married, but I knew you children would raise a fuss and say we hadn't known each other long enough, as if we're not both perfectly rational, sensible people who know what we're doing. And yesterday George said why not just go and do it, without any fanfare or telling everybody until afterward, and by the time we got back you'd be used to the idea— I know you'll like George when you meet him. So, my dears, we're going to Vegas to get married, and then we're going to fly to Paris for a honeymoon! George says I'm to get a whole new wardrobe in Paris! I can't tell you how excited and happy I am, really we both feel we've taken a new lease on life. Now, children, don't worry about anything, it's all going to be wonderful. I have paid all the utility bills, and there's nothing for you to do, except that I'll ask you to have the post office hold my mail, I forgot that until just now and there won't be time tomorrow. I was sorely tempted to tell Adele all about it when I saw her today, but managed to keep my guilty secret! We're just going to let it be a great surprise to everybody. We'll be flying back on New Year's Day, and the only thing we haven't decided is whether to live in my house or George's in La Cañada, but I think it will probably be George's. Now, my dears, don't worry, and I'll call you the minute we get back. All my love, Aunt Lila."

"Of all things to do!" said Carla Myrick. "Rushing off like that—"

Myrick said gloomily, "I just hope this man's all right."

Delia began to laugh. She laughed until her sides ached, and Varallo and O'Connor joined her. The Myricks just looked more aggrieved. "When I think," Delia gasped, "how we talked about it—so seriously—and of course she took her mink coat and all her jewelry—but not many clothes on account of the new wardrobe—when I *think* how we figured out what had happened to her—the Wash, and that engineer with his blueprints—and the f-f-fish—" She was reduced to helpless giggles.

"We just thought you ought to know," said Myrick stiffly. They got up and went out, Carla stuffing the letter back in her bag. Delia sat up and wiped her eyes, still giggling.

And Gonzales, coming in prodding a suspected heister in front of him, said, "What's the joke? And who wants to sit in on the questioning?"

On the Monday after Christmas, when Delia trailed in with Varallo at five-thirty after a busy day on a new homicide, O'Connor was sitting at Boswell's desk frowning thoughtfully. He said, "Listen, we've got a little problem. Eleven people want a kitten by the notes on the bulletin board, and we've only got four."

"First come, first served," said Varallo.

"But at least we've got a home for Mama cat, Burt's mother's going to take her."

"Oh, good," said Delia. "She's a nice cat, and such a good mother."

Mr. Beal came in to collect Rosie, and she trotted out with him amiably. Rosie was quite content to go home at night as long as she could spend her days at the police station.

"I am beat," said Varallo, yawning. "And there's more rain forecast. Another wet winter all right."

Delia drove home through heavy traffic, and just before she got to Riverside Drive, the rain started. It was coming down heavily as she turned onto Waverly Place, up to the big Spanish house. She slid the car into the garage, pulled down the big door, and went in through the service porch. She turned up the thermostat in the hall and went around switching on lights. As the light in the dining room came on, Henry woke up in his cage and gave her a loud wolf whistle, bouncing on his perch. "Hello, Henry," said Delia, and to her surprise and satisfaction Henry came right back at her.

"Hello, Delia dear! You're a very pretty girl, dear! Did you have a nice day? Say, let's all have a little drink!"

Delia burst out laughing. "You are an absurd creature," she told him. "But it's nice to have somebody to come home to."

ABOUT THE AUTHOR

Lesley Egan is a pseudonym for a popular, very prolific author of mysteries. Her most recent novels are *Little Boy Lost*, *Random Death*, and *The Miser*.